THE ROAD

THE GIRL IN THE PUB

Mark Leyland

CONTENTS

DEDICATED TO

MARK A SHANNON

13th March 1965 - 13th November 2019

THE BOOK'S MAIN CHARACTERS.

In LEIGH.

Adam = Book protagonist (Author of the main story)

Mark = Adam's best friend (also at Salford University with Adam)

Colin = Currently studying Economics at the University of Wales

Chris = Works at the DHSS in Leigh

Tony = Works at a Bank in Manchester

Paul = Works at an Accountancy firm in Leigh

Teabag = Friend of Paul's

Bev = Adam's major Love Interest

Eileen = Bev's best friend and love interest of Tony

Scarlett = Friend of Bev

Elaine = Adam's friend from Junior school.

Maria = Works with Tony at the Bank

Dave and Mick = Old friends of Adam (always in Britannia)

Charlie = Junior school friend of Adam (always in Britannia)

Patrick = Landlord of Britannia

In SALFORD.

Nick = Shares a flat with Adam and Mark (From Sheffield)

Mike = A Christian. Shares a flat with Adam and Mark (From Cheshire)

John = Friend of Adam on the same course. (From Wolverhampton)

Ian = Friend of Nick on the same course. Lives at Castle Irwell (From Liverpool)

Richard & Ron (Sharing with Ian at Castle Irwell)

Rob = Shares a flat with Adam, Mark and Nick in 3rd year, replacing Mike.

INTRODUCTION:
THE ROAD TO 1984

Sunday 1.00pm, Sept 2nd, 1984

It is a warm sunny day in early September as the plastic dials of my Philips clock radio flip indifferently over to 13.00. I put down my book and look out of the bedroom window. The window is slightly ajar, and I can hear children's laughter in the street and a yappy dog barking in the distance. My mum is in the garden hanging out some washing on the line and she notices me watching her. She smiles and gives me a four fingered baby wave to make me laugh and then goes back into the house to carry on with her chores. My dad has finished his weekly wash of the car and is now fiddling with something in the garage. I look around at the contents of my bedroom and see the small portable black and white television, the Toshiba music centre, bought for my 14th birthday, my record collection, and the books, hundreds of books, piled high on the shelves.

I think about the novel that I have just read; '1984' by George Orwell, his dystopian masterpiece written in 1948 and published in 1949, just one year before his death at the age of 46.

The book was completed three years after the end of World War 2 and warns of the dangers of a totalitarian government on a country's population and of the methods used to control society. Like his earlier novel, 'Animal Farm,' George Orwell was thought to be referring to Stalin's Soviet Union, but he could easily have been talking about the 3 Fascist dictators who had already heaped misery on a Europe, still crippled by the effects of war. Hitler's Germany and Mussolini's Italy had fought against the Allies during World War 2 while Franko's Spain had endured a civil war in which Orwell himself had joined the opposing Republican forces.

As Orwell was writing 1984, the threat of Hitler had been replaced by the fear of Soviet Communism, particularly in the United States, which was now competing with the Soviet Union to become the world's major power. Before the ink was dry on the Yalta and Potsdam Conferences, held in 1945, to determine what would happen at the end of the war, tensions were already high between the two countries. In Europe there was to be a new world order with Berlin, in Germany, to be divided amongst the Capitalist West and the Communist East. The dropping of 2 atomic bombs on Japan ended the war in the East but failed to guarantee a lasting world peace. In 1946 Churchill delivered his 'sinews of peace' speech which contained the famous phrase, 'an Iron curtain has descended on Europe'. The division in Europe and the opposing interests of East and West became known as 'The Cold War', a phrase that Orwell himself had coined. The mistrust between the Soviet Union and the United States was massive and is still a major concern in 1984.

Surprisingly, when Churchill delivered his famous speech in 1946, he was no longer the Prime minister of the U.K. It must have come as a huge shock to Winston Churchill and his fellow Conservatives to win the 2nd World War, only to lose the General Election to the Labour Party on the 5^{th of} July 1945.

My Grandad was a Labour Party supporter prior to the second world war and after fighting against the Germans and Italians, voted for Clement Atlee to take the UK forward into a brighter future for the working classes. Like Orwell, his political heroes had been the likes of Kier Hardie, Ramsay McDonald and Arthur Henderson, who had all gained prominence in the early 20th century, despite their working-class upbringings. However, Orwell had become an idealist, obsessed with political utopia, and lost interest in the Labour Party, in favour of Democratic Socialism. He had little interest in what the working classes were demanding after World War 2, but that wasn't surprising, considering his father had been a wealthy country gentleman and owner of Jamaican plantations, while Orwell labelled himself as 'lower-upper-middle class. Equally, when the war was won, my grandfather wasn't overly concerned about Stalin and Totalitarian Dictatorships. He was more interested in his own future and the plight of his fellow working classes and backed his cause by becoming a local Labour councillor, in Leigh. In '1984', Orwell referred to the working classes as 'Proles' who were considered irrelevant by the novel's ruling party. The book's major protagonist, Winston Smith, stated that 'if there is hope, (for a revolution) it lies with the proles', but 'Big Brother' wasn't concerned about them as they had no political consciousness and were too thick to matter. In truth, prior to 1945, the working classes had largely been irrelevant, unless a major war came along, in which case they were required to do their patriotic duty and fight for King and country. Too much economic power was in the hands of too few men and the Labour Party Manifesto intended to change this.

The working-classes demanded a plentiful supply of good food, useful work to be proud of, and comfortable labour-saving homes that took advantage of the resources of modern science and productive industry. They wanted a higher standard of living, security for all, and an education system that would give every child an opportunity to develop into their best self. Victory in World War 2 meant that the working-classes now had a voice, and they used it to demand the better, brighter, future that they were now entitled to. They sought a complete overhaul of the U.K, a programme of modernisation of its homes, an investment into its factories and machinery, its schools and its Social Services and full employment with good wages. There were to be no depressed areas in the new Britain. It was to look after the health of the nation and its children, provide Social Insurance against a rainy day and build a world of peace and progress.

It was the formation of the National Health Service in 1948 that went down as one of the Labour Party's greatest achievements and it was another of my Grandad's heroes that contributed significantly to its success. Aneurin Bevan was the Labour Party's Minister of Health from 1945-51. He was born into a working-class family in South Wales and was one of ten children of a Coal mining father and seamstress mother. He left school at 13, having achieved little academic success and worked as a Butcher's boy before beginning work as a miner. He had a stammer as a child and developed nystagmus, but he joined the Labour Party after World War 1 and gained a reputation as a good orator. In 1928 he won a seat on Monmouthshire County council and was elected as an M.P the following year. At 47 he became the youngest member of Clement Attlee's cabinet and was unfortunate not to become Labour leader when Attlee retired in 1955. When he died of stomach cancer at only 62 years, he had contributed significantly to the post war political landscape.

By 1948, life was gradually improving for the working classes, who had started to gather in flourishing communities centred around profitable manufacturing industries such as coal mining, car production and the iron and steel industry. The Labour government nationalised the country's major industries and focused on a programme of rebuilding the city's destroyed by war. A period of sustained economic growth followed, and the working classes developed a strong cultural identity to be proud of. In Central Europe, the French, UK and USA partitions of Germany were merged to form West Germany. The Soviet Union responded by cutting off all road and rail links so that Western Berlin had no access to food supplies and faced starvation.

On April 14th, 1949, the USA and Canada, along with 10 western European countries, formed NATO (North Atlantic Treaty Organisation), in response to the perceived growing threat posed by the Soviet Union. The treaty worked on the premise of a collective defence, which meant that any attack against one of the allies was an attack against all. On August 29th, 1949, the Soviets responded by successfully testing their first nuclear device, thus becoming the second country to possess nuclear capability. When North Korea invaded South Korea in June 1950 George Orwell had already passed away, and by the time that the war had ended in July 1953, 'with the North affiliated with Russia and the South affiliated with the USA', Stalin had died, to be succeeded by Nikita Khrushchev. Great Britain by this point had become the third country to acquire nuclear capability.

The Communist East raised the stakes further on May 14th, 1955, when the Warsaw Pact was formed to counteract the formation of NATO, with member states including East Germany, Poland, Hungary, Romania, Bulgaria, Czechoslovakia, Albania and the Soviet Union. Despite this move, not all was well amongst the Eastern states and on October 23rd, 1956, the Hungarian Revolution began in Budapest, as a protest to Communist rule. The following day Soviet tanks entered Budapest. Despite a new Hungarian government being formed that introduced freedom of speech and freedom of religion, Hungary fell to the Soviets on 10th November 1956.

In 1957 the Soviet Union and the USA found another way to flex their muscles when Sputnik 2 carried Laika the dog into space, thus beginning the Space Race between the two countries. This was followed on April 12th, 1961, by Russian cosmonaut, Yuri Gagarin, becoming the first human being in space. 5 days later, a force of Cuban exiles, trained by the CIA and backed by the American government, attempted to invade Cuba and overthrow the Communist government of Fidel Castro. The attack, which became known as the 'Bay of Pigs' invasion, was an embarrassing failure for the United States. However, 18 months later, Cuba was once more in the news when a U.S spy plane spotted the construction of a Soviet nuclear missile base, and President J.F Kennedy demanded the Russians withdrawal, on threat of war. Fortunately, the Soviets agreed to remove the weapons and war was averted. J.F.K was assassinated the following year.

At the time of the J.F.K assassination my dad was courting my Mum and when Leonid Brezhnev replaced Nikita Khrushchev as Soviet leader on October 15th, 1964, I was one month old. If you ask my dad what he was doing at the time of the Cuban missile crisis or the Kennedy assassination, he can't remember. He had his football and his Elvis quiff to think about, his office job at Joshua Tetley's brewery and his next date with my mum. By the time 'Mr eyebrows' became leader of Russia, he was worrying about money, a better job, a new car, clothes for the baby and somewhere to live.

The family lived with my Grandparents for 18 months until we moved to our own terraced house in Overton Street in Leigh. By then, the Vietnam war had begun, and my dad had become a window cleaner.

I heard about the Soviet troops' invasion of Afghanistan on 24th December 1979, on the television news and I can remember that the U.S and UK made a strong public denunciation of the invasion. I can also remember Ronald Reagan becoming President of the USA, his blossoming relationship with Margaret

Thatcher and his policy of 'détente', which planned to roll back Soviet influence in the Soviet bloc countries.

In 1980 the United States boycotted the Moscow Olympics, in protest against the Soviet invasion of Afghanistan, along with 65 other countries. Personally, I was pleased that Great Britain decided to attend the games as I had high hopes for Sebastian Coe, Steve Ovett and Daley Thompson and thought that Sharon Davies looked good in a bathing suit. The Soviet Union was to return the complement 4 years later when 14 Eastern Bloc countries boycotted the Los Angeles Summer Olympics.

In March-April 1983 the U.S navy conducted the largest fleet exercise held since WW2 in the North Pacific, with 40 ships, 23000 crew members and 300 aircraft. The purpose of the mission was to intentionally provoke the Soviet Union into responding, so that the U.S forces could study their response, tactics and capabilities. The exercise was successful but relations between the two countries were severely strained, with tensions reaching their highest levels since the Cuban missile crisis of 1962. Then, on 26th September, the nuclear early warning radar of the Soviet Union reported the launch of an intercontinental ballistic missile from bases in the United States. Stanislav Petrov, who was on duty at the Soviet command centre of the early warning system, suspected a false alarm and decided not to relay the warning up the chain of command to the current Soviet leader, Yuri Andropov. The system had malfunctioned, and Petrov's brave decision probably prevented a retaliatory attack and an escalation to a full- scale nuclear war.

By September 1983, I had passed my A Levels and was preparing for university life in Salford, but my main story begins a year later, on September 2nd, 1984, thirty-nine years after the end of World War 2 and the start of the Cold War. The Soviet Union is still the biggest threat to peace in Europe and the Cold War continues, but what about life for the working classes in 1984 and what has become of the Labour Party and Orwell s concerns regarding Totalitarianism in the U.K?

CHAPTER 1:
LIFE IN A NORTHERN TOWN
Sunday 3.00pm, Sept 2nd, 1984

Hello reader, my name is Adam, and this is my story. I am a 19-year-old History and Economics student at Salford University, due to begin my 2nd year studies in five weeks' time. I am 6 foot 2" tall and slim, with dark black hair and a sexy pair of hips.

I haven't achieved much in my life to date and wouldn't say that I was remarkable at any one thing. I have never had a real job or owned my own home. I have never owned a car despite passing my driving test on St Patrick's Day last year. I have never been abroad, and I have yet to fall in love. I voted for the first time, last June, but that was a fucking waste of time.

Ok, I'm still only 19, but Nigel Short, who also lives in Leigh, became a chess Grandmaster this year and he's younger than me. If I do have a talent, it is for reading. I love to read and have done so for most of my life. If it wasn't for having to read Jane Austen for my English Literature A Level, I may even have gone on to study English Literature at University. Fortunately, for me, Jane Austen died at just 41 years of age, having only completed 6 novels. Having read her books and scrutinized all aspects of her life for two years, I can only assume that she died of boredom, waiting hopelessly for Mr Darcy to sweep her off her feet. As a result of my reading, I have developed many strong views and opinions about our world, but my main priority at the present time, is getting laid.

I was born in 1964 in Leigh, Lancashire, a northern mining town about 14miles west of Manchester, 10 miles west of Salford, 9 miles southwest of Bolton and 7 miles southeast of Wigan. Liverpool is about 24 miles west of Leigh, along the East Lancashire Road that connects it to Manchester. I am giving you this useful information because these places have accounted for about 99% of my life to date. I was going to draw a map to give the locations some perspective, but I'm not a cartographer, and I couldn't be arsed.

I was brought up as an only child, by a loving mother and a football mad father. My mother works nights at Astley Hospital as an auxiliary nurse, while my father is a Window Cleaner. My mother knew Georgie Fame when she was a young girl, but he was Clive Powell back then, living in Cotton Street in Leigh and he wasn't famous. Soon after I came along, we lived in a terraced house in a cul-de-sac which backed onto a factory called Wallpaper Supplies. Environmentally, it wasn't the worst place in the U.K to live, but it wasn't the best either. As a young boy, I knew all the names and faces of the neighbours that lived in our street. It was a street enriched with kind warm-hearted, hard-working families and I felt safe and happy living there. There was a wonderful community spirit, where one family could be seen supporting another family on a regular basis. Whether it was by looking after the kids, mowing a lawn, walking the dog, baking a cake or erecting a fence, the community pulled together. It was as if there was an invisible bartering process in place, but no-one was keeping count. This wonderful 'all in it together' approach also transferred itself through to the children. It would not be unusual to see large groups of kids of all ages, walking together through the woods, into the fields, and along the canal bank miles from home. It was simply how things were and no-one blinked an eye. We would climb trees, build bonfires, make dens and play hide and seek in old- abandoned warehouses, only returning home when it started to get dark.

Despite our feral existence, we were pretty- well behaved, respected our elders and lived a magical life. In addition, I also had my books and to everyone's surprise passed my 11+ examination and went to a grammar school in Bolton. Initially, nothing much changed for me. I had tried, but disliked smoking by the age of 10, enjoyed a beer at 12 and lost my virginity on my 14th birthday. I have purposefully never tried illegal drugs, hard or soft.

Leigh is the centre of my world, and it is a working-class town justly proud of its heritage. Once linked historically with agricultural and dairy farming, it became better known for domestic spinning and weaving which resulted in a successful silk and cotton industry. The mining of coal soon followed and when Leigh became connected to the canals and railways, it became a major industrial town.

Leigh is a Rugby town whose most recent claim to fame came in 1982 when its Rugby League team won the Championship trophy for the first time since

1906. Many of my school friends skipped out of 6th form college to support them during a tense 13-4 victory at Whitehaven on the last day of the season, to clinch the trophy. As a result of this major event for the town, the names of manager, Alex Murphy, and players such as captain John Woods and the magnificent Des Drummond, will forever be celebrated in Leigh for temporarily bringing back its glory years. Alex Murphy was the captain of Leigh when we beat Leeds to win our 2nd Challenge Cup in 1971, so we have much to thank him for, and it was great to put one over the 'Pie Eaters,' who hadn't won the Championship trophy since 1960, or the Challenge Cup since 1965. Residents of Leigh often feel like second class citizens as part of the Metropolitan Borough of Wigan. We sadly, lost our Railway station in 1969 and while this had nothing to do with Wigan, it is always nice to be able to blame someone.

3 months after my 14th birthday my parents moved us to Pennington and things were never quite the same for me. It was December 1978, and we entered the so called 'winter of discontent,' and 6 months later in June 1979 Margaret Thatcher came to power.

Pennington was a more prosperous part of Leigh and even the 14 years old me could see that. It meant moving away from my old group of friends, albeit closer to my wealthier grammar school friends, who also lived in Pennington. Unfortunately, there was no equivalent sense of community amongst my new neighbours. Indeed, we rarely spoke to them and didn't get to know anyone's name on the street we now lived on. I was never sure whether it was a 'class thing' or just a different way of people existing together. At our previous house we were among similar working- class families like miners, bricklayers and labourers, who were proud of their roots. It felt to me as though these people were trying to escape their roots by striving for something more respectable.

My day-to-day life had changed, and I no longer felt secure or comfortable in my new environment. I started to feel alienated and became anxious and disorientated by my surroundings. I didn't feel valued. I didn't feel worthwhile. I didn't belong. Over the next couple of years, I became troubled by feelings of dread and despair as I attempted to make sense out of where life was taking me. I quickly rejected religion. Going to a Roman Catholic school and being taught by priests helped with that. I became suspicious of Capitalism and most forms of authority. Reading 'Das Capital' by Karl Marx may have helped with that one! Whatever I was being told by my teachers, priests and politicians and other representatives of the 'establishment' no longer reflected my own interpretation of the world.

It was only when I became interested in the works of Soren Kierkegaard and John Paul Sartre last year that things became clearer, and I began to wonder whether I had been suffering from a mild case of teenage 'existential angst'. John Paul Sartre once said that 'everything has already been figured out, except how to live' and so I started to consider how I wanted to live my life, in order to give it meaning. Instead of being led by the mentality of the pack, I decided to take control and make my own decisions on what was going to be important in my life and the values I would choose to live it.

Fortunately, during my struggles at the age of 14, I did have a wonderful friend called Mark who I had known since we were children. Our mothers were both nurses and became good friends, resulting in Mark and I spending a lot of time together as kids. Just by being there, he probably kept me sane at a time when I felt lost and insecure about myself and my life. I sometimes wonder how things might have turned out for me if it wasn't for Mark, who became my one constant companion during this difficult period.

Mark had a sister and a dog called Sandy. She was a strange looking thing, the dog, not his sister, but she seemed to like me, and I loved dogs. I'd never owned a dog, but I used to take Zebedee, the next door's Golden Labrador for walks before we moved to Pennington, and I adored him. By then, I'd already noticed that most animals seemed to like and trust me, which I couldn't say about people. Maybe that's my fault, as I can be overly suspicious and cautious about a person when I first meet them and prefer to work out what they are all about first. I don't like selfish self- centred people who are cocky and over-confident and mostly talk shit, and there are an awful lot of them about. Have a think, you might be one yourself. I usually prefer it when a person is initially modest and quiet, but then surprises me with some amazing talent that they have kept hidden away from the world. In contrast, you usually know where you are with animals. If they love you, they will love you forever and ask little in return. I think if I were an animal, I would be more popular than I am as a person.

At the time, it may have appeared to family and acquaintances that my insecurities at 14-16 were due to the normal process of growing-up from child to young adult. They may have decided that I was starting to worry about the future prospect of finding a job and a career. It now seems probable that my issues were more to do with existing in a meaningless world. However, as an angry 14-year-old boy, I blamed Margaret Thatcher.

From 1979 my world had changed from one that felt happy and safe to one that now seemed very scary. From a loquacious, self-confident, happy go lucky boy, I had turned into a frightened, introverted, sulky young man, who only had his books to placate him. To make matters worse, it wasn't usually a schoolbook that I was reading and as the impending threat of my O levels loomed onto the horizon, I realised that I was going to need to do something that I had never done before. 'Revision'. The prospect scared me, especially when I came to realise that all the other kids at my grammar school had been doing this for the past 3 or 4 years. I also came to understand that 'coasting' wasn't necessarily a comment on my school report that I should be proud of.

Despite focusing more on my school- work and quickly improving my grades, I sometimes feel that I regressed mentally between the age of 14 and 16 as I blindly attempted to resolve my issues. I don't think it helped that I was being educated at an all-boys school, after previously spending a lot of time with girls, or that I had grown at an alarming rate, to develop into a tall skinny young man. Thankfully, success with my O Levels and A Levels and achieving a place at university did help with my confidence issues, while the chest expanders also contributed. I had boldly done what my teachers had asked of me and 'pulled my socks up.'

However, these were still painful years for me, and what genuinely improved my self- confidence, was going to the pub on a regular basis, when I turned 17 years old. This was an accepted part of the culture of the working- classes and a rite of passage for my community. While I still felt like a 'fish out of water' in my educational environment, sitting in an old-fashioned working-class pub with a pint in my hands, chatting with some of the locals, added meaning to my life and made me feel as though I was back home. The locals included some of my friends and neighbours from when life seemed much simpler. They largely remain friendly, salt of the earth people, although some of them have changed. In 1984, there is now a sadness and underlying bitterness in some of them which can result in tears when they are drunk. It is never pleasant to watch a grown man cry.

As a working-class boy growing up in the North of England, I was starkly aware that my family and friends were politically powerless. The current U.K government's control and manipulation over the working classes isn't dramatically different to other governments in Europe and throughout the World. All governments control their population using techniques of fear and manipulation, but democratic governments tend to do it more subtly than the dictators. They are more cunning, crafty, ingenious, inventive and clever. They are devious bastards, so beware.

In 1979, Margaret Thatcher showed her face to the electorate and the UK finally had its very own dictator. It wasn't 'Big Brother' our generation had to worry about, it was 'Big Sister'. My grandparents and parents had their own struggles to deal with in the 1940s and 1960s, respectively, but ever since Margaret Thatcher marched onto the political stage, the clock seems to have been turned back 40 years to 1939 as far as the working classes are concerned. On examining Orwell's future political concerns raised in '1984,' they don't reflect my own current experience of life in the UK, but I'm just a thick prole. While I am concerned about the threat of nuclear war and still see Russia as the biggest threat to peace in Europe, I am more worried about events and politics in my own country. I want to celebrate my community with family and friends, receive a good education, maintain equality with the middle and upper classes, travel widely and enjoy a happy and healthy life with a sexy wife and a good job. Unfortunately, despite the improvements made following the war, inequalities are still rife in the U.K and working- class success is again being hampered by the government. Standards of living, access to housing, health services and education have improved over the past 39 years but there are still huge differences between rich and poor, and I think these differences are only going to get worse, now that Margaret Thatcher is in power.

Since 1945 Leigh folk have always voted for the Labour Party when the elections come around, and last year they obtained a 25% majority, despite another Tory victory in the General Election. They are not fans of Margaret Thatcher and her all-male cabinet, and there are serious concerns about her dislike of Trade Unions and what she is currently doing to the Mining Industry. In Leigh we currently have the Parsonage and Bickershaw pits open and there is something comforting about seeing the giant wheel and chimneys on the town's skyline.

Now, we can only watch in horror at events taking place in South Yorkshire and despise Margaret Thatcher and the Conservatives for the misery they are inflicting on hundreds of hard-working families and for the devastating impact this is having on previously strong communities. It feels as though Margaret Thatcher has been planning this attack on the working-classes for years and we are now witnessing a deliberate attempt to destroy its communities forever. In 1974, she would have been 'spitting feathers' when the Miners' strike brought down the Edward Heath government, and ten years later she is determined that her government doesn't meet the same fate. In 1974, Arthur Scargill became a hero to many working -class people by successfully using 'flying pickets' to target certain plants and prevent the transportation of coal. He is attempting to use the same tactic in 1984, but Margaret Thatcher is better prepared than Edward Heath was, and this time it's personal. She isn't content to merely win the battle with the miners and is instead targeting their permanent destruction, mercilessly sticking in the knife, until they have no more fight left in them. Arthur Scargill is beginning to realise this, but he has been outgunned and is powerless to stop her. In 1984, he is being cast as the villain in the daily news bulletins and is losing popular support amongst some of the working classes, while Margaret Thatcher is winning the public relations battle. In Leigh, however, we can see through her cunning and manipulative ways, and no matter what she has achieved by winning the Falklands War or whatever future success she has with the economy, she will always be despised in these parts. She has already used her powers to demote several of her free-thinking opponents, in favour of her own supporters, and made her government increasingly centralised at the expense of local government, making her significantly more powerful than any of her predecessors in government.

As a 14-year-old boy starting to show a morbid interest in politics, I can vividly remember the Saatchi and Saatchi 'Britain isn't working' slogan, quickly followed by the 'Labour isn't working' slogan, used by the Conservatives for the 1979 General Election campaign. Well, that's all well and good, but it wasn't fucking working two years later when the Tories were in power, and I was a 16-year-old boy, looking at the jobs market for the first time. In the 1930's Norman Tebbit's dad got on his bike to look for work, but he wasn't from 'round here'. On 2nd June, last year, I voted for Michael Foot and the Labour Party, only to see Margaret Thatcher record a Landslide majority of 144 seats. This of course, was largely on account of her decisive victory in the Falklands conflict between April 2nd and June 14th, 1982, when she was supported by friend and fellow dictator, General Augusto Pinochet of Chile. As a 17-year-old sixth former, at the time, I knew that the Falklands were close to Argentina, but I had to look it up on the map to find it.

Unfortunately, it now seems as though Margaret Thatcher will be in power until 1987 at least, and the Labour Party need to appoint a strong leader to break the Conservatives dominance. Michael Foot wasn't the man to do it despite his obvious intelligence and I'm certain that Neil Kinnock will never be elected Prime minister, for as long as I have a hole in my arse. There is a young man named John Smith who looks promising as a future leader of the Labour Party, so I'm hoping that it will be in better shape in a couple of years. Whether Leigh will still be in a reasonable state by then is anybody's guess. It already has a stink of death about it and with many of its traditional industries now under threat, I shudder to think what the future might hold. My father has friends that work for Ward and Goldstone and the Cable-works, where I hear that the threat of redundancy is again looking ominous for two more of Leigh's major employers.

My Grandad often reminisces about his hopes and concerns in 1945, following the end of World War 2 and believes that the time has now come for the younger generation to re-discover their voice, in order to improve the future of the battered working-classes of the United Kingdom. However, much of the damage has already been done and even my best friends don't seem to care about Politics, while those that do, now have a more middle-class outlook on life. Labour leaders have also become more middle class and it won't be long before the lines are blurred between what a Conservative politician and a Labour Politician should look like. In 1977, the Stranglers sang about 'No more Heroes' and this seems to be the case as far as the Working Classes are concerned. While optimism was justified in 1948 things are looking very bleak for the working-classes in 1984. Unfortunately, it now takes a 'silver spoon' to make a difference to our world and it might be time to look elsewhere for our heroes. There isn't currently an Aneurin Bevan or Kier

Hardie amongst our politicians and both men would surely be appalled at the current plight of the working classes in 1984.

Sadly, the writing is on the wall for Leigh and similar working- class towns in Lancashire and Yorkshire and my friends and I will need to adapt if we don't want to become part of another 'Lost Generation'. With our industries and communities left decimated, the South of England seems to be largely unaffected by the closing down sale currently taking place in the North, and we are now facing a 'divide' that is so great, that we could be living in two different nations.

CHAPTER 2.
THE GIRL IN THE PUB.
Sunday Evening, September 2nd, 1984.

Undaunted by the current predicament of my town; tonight, I am about to go on the piss again with my five Grammar school friends, who also live in Leigh. Like me, Mark and Colin are at university and have one month of holiday left before returning to their studies. Mark is at Salford University with me and this year we will be sharing a flat with two other lads. Colin is at the University of Wales studying Economics. My other friends are Chris, Tony, and Paul, who all decided to look for work after A- Levels, rather than pursue a university education. Chris is a year older than the rest of us and has been working for the DHSS for the past 12 months, while Tony works in a Bank in Manchester. Paul has been unemployed for the past 12 months but has recently started a new position as a Trainee Accountant at a firm in Leigh.

While Leigh is sometimes described as a dirty old industrial town, it does have lots of good pubs and a decent nightclub. Most of its pubs are old fashioned drinking establishments for the working- class man, and for me that is part of the attraction. Unfortunately, a few wine bars have recently started to open selling expensively shit tasting beer, adorned with palm trees and bright flashing lights. The 'Tropics' is one of these trendy new 'drinking shops' and we will probably drop in at some point tonight, not to admire the ambience of the place, but because it attracts pretty girls with big hair and shiny white teeth, wearing sexy boots and a tiny piece of fashionable cloth to protect their modesty.

We have a tried and tested route to follow that allows for occasional diversions should this be deemed necessary, but we always start and usually finish at the Britannia pub. After a few beers at the Britannia, we walk up and over the famous Bridgewater Canal into town. The Canal was opened in 1761 from Worsley to Manchester, and later extended from Manchester to Runcorn, and then from Worsley to Leigh. It also connects to the Rochdale Canal, Trent and Mersey Canal, Leeds and Liverpool Canal and the Manchester Ship Canal, which ends at the Salford and Manchester Docks. Sadly, the Docks closed in 1982 and were purchased by Salford City Council last year. It remains to be seen what their plans are to redevelop the area.

We will call in for a cider at the 'Moonraker' or a bottle of beer at the 'Tropics', depending on our mood. This is followed by the George and Dragon, the Boars Head and maybe the Musketeer, if Mark gets his way. The Pied Bull comes next, which is another one for the ladies, but without the palm trees and flashing lights, before moving on to the Courts Hotel and the Globe. This may sound like a lot of pubs for a Sunday evening, but they are closely- packed together, and we can get very thirsty doing all that walking.

I like to dress well when I go into Leigh, and on this mild and pleasant September evening I am wearing some light grey trousers, grey slip- on shoes, with no socks and a mauve and grey flowery short sleeved shirt, just in case we go to the Tropics.

I set off from home at 7.30 to cover the one mile walk to the 'Brit'. We go there to chew the fat and whet our whistles for an hour before launching ourselves on the town. We meet at the Britannia because it is spacious and comfortable and quiet enough to have a decent conversation, before starting our evening. The décor is very 1970's and some of the furniture is very 'brown' and could do with an update, but the natives are friendly, and it has a decent jukebox. There is a Lounge area where we congregate and a Tap Room at the other side of the bar, where most of the older customers sit to play dominoes. There is also a dart board and a pool table situated to the right of the men's toilets. The ladies' toilets are in the Lounge. The pub is popular among the young and the old, and you will see an assortment of folk from 3 'generations' mixing amicably together. The main connecting factor is that they all come from a working-class background. All are keen to chat about any subject you might wish to discuss, all are courteous and polite, and all have a story to tell, usually with a large alcoholic drink waving about in their hands. Only the younger generation venture into town and most of the clientele will still be there at last orders to welcome them back to the pub. I feel a great affection for all these people, even if some of them do get a bit 'lairy' later in the evening.

The landlord is an Irishman named Patrick and he has run pubs for the whole of his working life, and he is incredibly good at it. He knows how to create a good atmosphere in the pub, he knows his regulars and what their requirements are, and he keeps his eyes on the non-regulars. He has a good singing voice and is always ready to launch himself into a medley of Irish songs to encourage a sing along. This kind of night usually results in a lock-in, whereby only the back door of the pub remains unlocked, allowing his regulars to enter or exit the pub as they please. I don't know if Patrick knows members of the local constabulary, but I don't think he's ever been raided by the police. Patrick is in his mid-fifties with black and silver thinning hair and a beer belly, but he is still capable of throwing out an unruly customer if he needs to. He has a long-suffering wife called Sandra, and a grown -up daughter named Shirley.

I arrive at the Brit at 7.45 to see Mark already at the bar talking to Patrick. He has a fresh pint of Guinness in his hand, and I don't think that it's his first. He turns to greet me with his cheeky lopsided grin and asks me what I'm having to drink. Mark is shorter than me but more solidly built. His hair is long, black and unruly and he is sporting a 'tash' and stubble on his chin. Mark is probably the cleverest person I know and is studying Electrical Engineering at University. He is wearing his customary blue jeans and a black tee-shirt with a Band name emblazoned on the front, with dates and venues of concerts on the back. Today, its Black Sabbath, a band Mark and I went to watch together at the Manchester Apollo in 1980. That night, Ronnie James Dio did a superb job of singing Black Sabbaths back catalogue of songs, but for us, there will only ever be one Ozzy Osbourne. Back then, we loved our heavy metal bands and the emerging punk scene and had record collections that included AC/DC, Motorhead, Rainbow, the Scorpions, Rush, the Stranglers, Sex Pistols, the Boomtown Rats and the wonderful Buzzcocks, whose singer songwriter, Pete Shelley, was born in Milton Street in Leigh in 1955.

While Mark has remained committed to Heavy Rock and still attends such concerts on a regular basis, I now favour some newer bands, like the Smiths, the Cure, REM, and 'James' who are a local up and coming band, who I expect to make it big very soon. I step up to the bar and see Marks faded denim jacket lying on a bar stool and I order a pint of Lager from Patrick. The beer is another good reason for starting proceedings at the Brit, as you can always rely on Patrick to pull you a tasty thirst- quenching pint.

I wave to Dave and Mick who are sitting in the Tap Room with a couple of old blokes who are playing dominoes. The old blokes' names are Peter and Stuart, and they are both wearing old three -piece suits, tie and overcoat and a flat cap, as they probably have for most of their adult lives. Dave and Mick are brothers who I used to 'knock about with' as a boy, before moving to Pennington. Dave is a couple of years older than Mick and is Black while Mick is White. They have both worked on the bins since leaving school at 15 or 16. Their mother had 3 boys with 3 different fathers. The youngest, Wayne, died 3 years ago when he drowned in the canal, while being chased by the police over a minor offence he had committed. Mick is my age and was a good cricketer when we were 14, but he was a fast bowler and had to stop playing a few years ago due to a shoulder injury he picked up on the bins.

Colin walks into the pub and gives us the nod as he makes his way to the bar.

"Get you both another one" he says.

Yeah, "Guinness and a Lager", Mark replies.

Like me, Colin is tall, slim and dark, but perhaps a couple of inches shorter. He is a quiet lad but has a wicked sense of humour and is also a big fan of the Smiths. Like most of the lads, he is a big Rugby fan, and the conversation will now change to the latest Rugby League and Rugby Union news, including which players are flavour of the month, which ones are past their prime and who should be selected for the next tour of South Africa, New Zealand or Australia, not that I am usually listening at this point. I leave Mark and Colin to their conversation and go to see what I can put on the jukebox. While I am always keen to see Leigh Rugby League do well, my passion is Football, and Manchester United in particular. I have supported them since 1970 when they had become a team in decline. Bobby Charlton and Dennis Law were past their best and while George Best was still performing at the highest level, he was beginning to develop other interests. I went through the disappointment of relegation to the 2nd division while most of my friends switched their support, first to Leeds United and then to Liverpool, as children tend to do when their team is losing every week. They returned to Division One the following year, but despite a couple of FA Cup victories, they have never really threatened to win the League and 17 years have now passed since their last League title. Mark and I will be going back to Old Trafford in a few weeks to see what they can do this season, but we have learned to limit our expectations.

I make my music selections and hear Johnny Marrs opening guitar riff to 'What difference does it make' jangling through the pub speakers.

"Good choice", shouts Colin.

I look towards the bar and see that Tony and Chris have arrived.

"Top up", shouts Tony.

"Two Lagers and a Guinness" Mark replies.

Chris informs us that Paul is already out in Leigh with his friend Teabag and will meet us for a drink at the Pied Bull later. We don't know why his friend is called Teabag but he's a friendly lad with a big personality that matches his physique. Paul met him at the gym last month, where he has been spending time on his new body building regime. Paul has red hair and looks and walks a bit like 'shaggy' from Scooby Doo, so he is trying to build some muscle onto his slender frame. Teabag has already achieved that muscle and is built like a Tank. He works as a Butcher during the day and does a bit of Bouncing work at the weekend, no doubt hoping that he can break some bones, if it all kicks off at the club. We have heard that he has something of a chequered past, but we haven't yet asked him what this involves. Every time we meet Teabag, he challenges me to an arm wrestle because he has heard from Paul that I am quite strong. Personally, I think he just wants to try and snap my arm off. His other claim to fame is his tattoo which is on the right cheek of his bum and consists of a pair of bright red lips with an angry looking penis sticking out between them. For some reason it always makes me think of the opening credits to the film version of the Rocky Horror Picture Show. I watched this film for the first time, last year, after returning home 'bladdered' after a Saturday night out. Following the film's opening scenes and the songs 'Sweet Transvestite' and 'The Time Warp' I was convinced that someone had slipped something into my drink. I could have sworn that later in the film, I saw the 'Bat out of Hell' singer 'Meatloaf' being attacked by the sweet transvestite with an axe, but I could have been dreaming at that point. I'm not sure whether there is a hidden meaning behind Teabag's tattoo, but I am honoured to have been shown it on every occasion we have met so far. Teabag comes from an Irish background and has a trace of an Irish accent, but he's been living in Leigh now for 6 years. He has dyed blond spiky hair and a little toothbrush moustache, dresses impeccably in designer gear and smells of Mandate. Paul, by contrast, can often look like a 'scruff bag'. Chris tells us that they are going to Brighton in a couple of weeks to stay with one of Teabags cousins. Apparently, Brighton is the place to party these days.

Tonight, we visit the Tropics, George and Dragon and the Boars Head, before arriving at the Pied Bull at around 9.45pm. I go to the bar and notice Elaine with a group of girls, standing near the pub stairs. Elaine is a lovely girl, who Mark, and I were at Junior school with. She is small and pretty with short brown hair and is wearing an attractive figure- hugging blue dress. I know some of her friends but can't help noticing one that I haven't seen before. She is tall and skinny with long auburn hair and a shapely pair of legs. She notices me looking over and smiles at me. She has beautiful dark brown eyes and is wearing a red and black top which appears to be concealing a more than adequate pair of breasts, for such a slim girl. I order our drinks and walk over to say hello to Elaine, but my eyes are still drawn towards the mystery girl. Elaine has booked a skiing trip for Christmas time and is taking it easy tonight as she has an important meeting in the morning and her friend is a friend of a friend called Beverley. I make a beckoning sign to my friends to call them over and we begin a conversation with the whole group. This allows me to speak to Beverley who oozes confidence and isn't backward at coming forward. She is articulate and demonstrative and tells me she is due to begin her 3rd year at Liverpool University studying French and German. This year, she is doing her teaching experience and will be starting at a school near Paris, in France at the end of September, teaching English to a class of 16-year-old kids. After that, she will have one more year left at Liverpool University, before taking her teaching qualifications and becoming a teacher. I am already captivated by everything about her, and my head is starting to go a little dizzy. Fortunately, Bev is a comfortable conversationalist and allows me enough time to regain my composure. We talk until last orders, by which time my friends have already moved on and I have missed last orders at the Brit. As I walk Bev to the taxi rank, I know that I've got to see her again. Fortunately, I know of an event taking place at Leigh Squash club the following Friday and take my opportunity to ask her out.

"I am going to be there with Colin and Tony, so bring along a couple of friends" I add.

Without needing time to consider my kind offer, Bev confirms that she and her friends will be there, steps into her taxi and waves me goodbye. After informing the driver of her destination, she sits upright, composes herself and then blows me a kiss through the window and smiles.

CHAPTER 3.
DATE NIGHT.
Monday 3rd - Friday 7th September 1984

The following morning, I wake up with a minor hangover but feel a vibrant energy running through my veins. Last night's event has completely blown me away and I am re-running the meeting with Bev through my mind. I have had five short- term relationships with girls in the last 3 years, but this already feels as though it has greater potential, and we haven't even been on a date yet. So far, my record is three dates with a girl called Denise, who moved to Australia with her parents, shortly after I groped her breasts for the first time. The other four girls didn't manage to top my exploits with Denise, although Dawn's French kiss showed potential, until I found out that she was practising it with another boy. The next 5 days are going to feel like an exceptionally long time.

On Tuesday, I help my dad on his window cleaning round for a couple of days, to earn myself a few quid for beer money. Colin has been working for a builder for a few months while Mark has done some work as a hospital porter. If we want to go out on a regular basis we need to be earning and none of us expect hand- outs from our parents. My Dad likes to start early and during the summer months that means a 6 o'clock start. He is 42 years old and extremely fit for his age, and while I do the downstairs windows, he is up the ladder doing the upstairs. It's not an easy job to do, particularly in the winter months when the weather is freezing cold and you can't feel your fingers, but it's a good earner if you are prepared to work hard and it pays the bills.

On Wednesday evening I play 5 a side with Chris and some of his football mates. I'm not as skilful as I was in my younger teenage years, but I manage to hold my own amongst some far better players than me by playing as a sweeper and the last line of defence for our goalkeeper.

We call for a couple of drinks at the Brit after the game and I manage a quick catch up with Charlie, who is sitting on her own at the bar smoking a cigarette. Charlie Is another girl that Mark and I went to Junior school with, and she now works as an exotic dancer in Manchester, a role for which she is wonderfully equipped. We call her Blondie because of her likeness to Debbie Harry. She has an appalling taste in men which is a big shame because she has a heart of gold.

As the drinks arrive, I excuse myself and go to sit with Chris in our usual seats. Chris is the sportsman of the group. He was the captain of our grammar school football team and was selected to play for the county when he was 16. He reminds me of Chris Waddle from Newcastle United when he dips his shoulder and runs at the defence with the ball. Having played cricket with Chris, I also know what a terrific wicket keeper batsman he is. He dated a girl nicknamed 'Hot Jules' for 12 months when he was in the 6th form, but the relationship broke down when he became ill with Crohn's disease. He has since had a successful operation and is back playing football again. Chris is blond and athletically built and tends to catch the eye of the ladies when he is out, but like the rest of us, he doesn't have a girlfriend at the present time.

Following my night out with Chris on Wednesday, Thursday drags slowly, until Friday morning, when the clock seems to stop altogether. I can feel butterflies in my stomach and start to become full of nervous energy, so I finish off the excellent 'The Stand' by Stephen King. I think he is a good writer and can't understand why the critics seem to give him a hard time. It is a mystery to me that these very same critics will marvel over the books of Jane Austen, who lived her entire life without any hint of a scandal that could have tarnished or even enhanced her reputation. This can't be said of Stephen King if the stories of drink and drugs are to be believed. He has an amazing imagination that borders on insane. The book creates a believable scenario whereby 99.9% of the world's population are wiped out by a deadly virus, resulting in the survivors having to rebuild civilization while being faced with a good versus evil dilemma. As this virus scenario is entirely plausible, the book creates a tension that one of Jane Austen's summer balls cannot hope to match. As a student of 20th Century history, I am familiar with the 1919 Spanish flu epidemic that resulted in millions of deaths across Europe following the end of World War 1, so it is entirely possible that we could be faced with a more virulent strain in the future, that may result in the end of the human- race, as we know it. There could even be an evil genius living in the world today who is sat in a Chinese Laboratory and plotting to release a deadly strain of killer virus on mankind. But that is probably moving more towards Ian Fleming territory than Stephen King.

During the week, Manchester United drew their fourth consecutive League game to continue their slow start to the season, a 1.1 home draw with Chelsea. Not a good sign if they are to challenge for the title this season.

In other news, the Space Shuttle 'Discovery' landed on September 5th following its maiden test voyage. Discovery became the third operational orbiter to enter service and was preceded by Columbia and Challenger. Judith Resnik became only the second American woman in space after Sally Ride and fourth overall.

Finally, Friday evening arrives, and the 3 amigos meet at the Britannia pub at 7.00pm. I am wearing my black jeans with a plum- coloured jacket and matching shoes, white shirt and a loose red leather tie. Colin, who is 'togged out' in his blue jeans and short sleeved white shirt, says that I look like a thermometer. Tony, also in his blue jeans and short sleeved white shirt laughs and calls me a 'fucking puff'. I smile and tell them both to 'fuck off'. We have a couple of pints and decide to go to the Pied Bull for one more drink, before moving on to the Squash Club. On entering the Pied Bull, I say hello to Albert who is sitting on a stool at the far left of the bar, near the door. Albert is in his mid-

50's but looks 70 and is dressed in the same long dirty coat and trilby hat that he wears whatever the weather, whatever the occasion. He visits the pub every Friday night and rumour has it that he has done so for the past 10 years. He used to visit the pub with his friend Ernest, long before it was refurbished and started to attract a younger clientele. Unfortunately, Ernest died of cirrhosis of the liver about 5 years ago, but Albert continues to sit at the same end of the bar every Friday night, despite standing out 'like a sore thumb'. It was only earlier this year that I realised that the two friends would have been known as Bert and Ernie and this made me question the validity of parts of the story.

One snake bite later we present ourselves for inspection at Leigh Squash Club, where we notice that the girls have already arrived. To begin with, we choose to ignore them and go straight to the bar to get the beers in. At this point, the girls will no doubt be discussing how cool and manly we are, by appearing relaxed and in control of the situation. And so, after keeping them 'sweating' for half an hour, we wander casually over to do the introductions. I look at Bev dressed wonderfully in a blue and white summer dress and smile at her nervously. Bev's friends are Scarlett and Eileen. Eileen was at the Pied Bull last Sunday, but this is the first time that we have met Scarlett. Eileen is a small, timid looking girl with mousy hair and is wearing a black top and grey skirt. Scarlett is a confident red head and is wearing an orange blouse with red trousers while nonchalantly smoking a cigarette. Tony sits down next to Eileen and Colin strikes up a conversation with Scarlett, while I go to the bar with Bev. Bev compliments me and the lads for acting cool and sexy on our arrival at the club, but it quickly becomes obvious that she is taking the piss. Fortunately, she is only teasing us over our boyish behaviour and isn't at all angry. She is right to take the piss, of course, as all three of us are still naïve when it comes to making a good first impression with the ladies. It is immediately clear that Bev likes me, despite my initial clumsiness, but it is also evident that she is the one in charge. It would be fair to say that this has been a common theme in my limited love life, to date.

When I lost my virginity on my 14th birthday it was with a 15-year-old girl called Mandy who told me what to hold, what to press and where to put it. Then, when I was 18, I was seduced by a woman in her early 20s at a friend of a friend's birthday party. Don't get me wrong, this time I'd made the first move by getting her a drink and kissing her, but she was the one who had suggested going upstairs. I was happy enough kissing her sexy red lips and grappling with her large spongy breasts until she asked me somewhat bluntly -

"Are you going to fuck me, or what?"

I decided that I would give it a go and performed quite adequately by all accounts. Not that I ever saw her again, she took advantage of me and then just pissed off home.

Coach trips to Manchester and Wigan and School Discos in Bolton, provided further opportunities for a bit of light romance, but once the last dance is over and you've sucked one another's faces off, it's not as though you can carry on back at their parent's house. I thought University might improve matters, but apart from a

Polish girl on my Quantitative Economics course, there was no-one who interested me during my first year. Lacking confidence in myself, I decided that the sexy Polish girl was probably a good church going Catholic and wouldn't be interested in a skinny none believing Northerner.

After a few drinks Bev and I decide to dance, and I am delighted when 'Relax' by Frankie Goes to Hollywood is played, as it allows me to do my wavy arms dance. Bev is clearly impressed by my moves, but to stop me from making a fool of myself, puts her arms around my neck and kisses me gently on the lips. While the kiss is soft, her passion burns through to my mouth, and I feel the faintest touch of her tongue on mine. It feels wonderfully sexy, so I eagerly go back for seconds. It was without doubt the greatest kiss of my young life. The timing was good, the connection felt right, the moisture was perfect and the warmth of our breath coming together was orgasmic. Well, almost. I don't know if I fell in love at that precise moment in time, but by the end of the night, I was totally smitten with this gorgeous, delicious, creature. As we walked hand in hand from the Squash Club to the middle of Leigh, I couldn't keep my hands off her. We had to keep stopping so that I could kiss her again. The intensity of my passion was bursting out of me, and I couldn't let her go for even one second. For her part, Bev seemed to be loving the attention and was laughing as I fussed over her and told her that I wanted to gobble her up. It felt as though no-one else in the world existed and that we were the only two people that now mattered. I was high on life and felt on top of the world. That awful feeling that I didn't belong, was now gone. I was part of a couple; I was in love, and someone loved me, despite all my obvious faults. We arrived at the taxi rank like the previous Sunday, but I was no longer that same person. It was as though a remarkable transformation had occurred, I was a caterpillar transformed into a butterfly and I was about to take off. I arranged to call Bev on Saturday morning and went home to dream sexy dreams about her.

CHAPTER 4.
FALLING IN LOVE.
September 8th- October 7th, 1984.

By 11 o'clock on Saturday morning Bev and I were back in Leigh. We went to the George and Dragon pub and bought a couple of soft drinks, so that we could sit and stare at one another, while talking about the amazing connection that had taken place between us. It so happens that Tony had asked Eileen out, and that the four of us are going on a double date tonight. I think Scarlett had been too much for Colin to handle, so that relationship went no further.

Tony was another of my friends who liked his Rugby and tended to play at least one game of Rugby League or Rugby Union over the weekend. He is a solidly built lad with black curly hair, tree trunk legs and strong arms, and he can take care of himself. This is probably just as well because he can sometimes wind people up the wrong way. It's not deliberate, but he loves the banter like all Rugby lads do. Unfortunately, he is quite opinionated and likes to voice those opinions loudly. He would never start a fight, but equally he would never back down from one. After successfully passing his A- Levels I thought that he would utilise his skill set by joining the Police force, but he ended up with a job in a Bank. Tony was a fellow English Literature A- Level student and is also a big reader. He supports Manchester United but prefers Hilton Park to Old Trafford.

Following my brief date with Bev, I meet up with Mark and we devour a couple of tasty steak and kidney pies from Waterfield's bakers before catching the Football Bus to Old Trafford. We stand in the Stretford End watching Man United beat Newcastle United 5-0, to record their first victory of the season. It is also the first game that Mark and I have attended this season, so we are hoping that this will lead to an upturn in form and a run of victories. To celebrate, we have a pint at the Flemish Weaver pub in Salford, just off the East Lancashire Road, and catch up with each other on the week's events.

By 8 o'clock, I am back in Leigh, meeting up with Bev, Tony and Eileen for a few drinks, before going to the Steak House in Atherton for a meal. Bev is the centre of attention, while Eileen is shy, and says little to begin with. Eileen talks about her work in a Care Home and mentions the Church of England on a couple of occasions, so she is clearly religious. I know that Tony's family is also quite religious, so this isn't likely to put him off her.

Despite my Roman Catholic upbringing, I have long considered myself to be Agnostic or a Humanist depending on how the mood takes me. Embracing Sartre, once more.

'I believe in nothing.' 'Only my scepticism prevents me from being an atheist'.

I do understand why many people find comfort in religion and see the importance of having 'Faith', but

I struggle to make sense of why they don't question the hundreds of anomalies, that exist in all the world's religions. As a passionate non-believer and a trainee existentialist, I have familiarised myself with all the major religions; and can immediately see the hypocrisy behind what they preach. In most cases, a set of rules and beliefs have been recorded hundreds of years ago in order to educate or control people into following a path that is desirable for society. This often explains why many politicians embrace Religion in order to control their subjects using fear of hell and damnation to manipulate them when necessary. Unfortunately, many of these rules and beliefs are no- longer relevant thousands of years later, now that the world has developed and moved on. People will be required to adopt 'Doublethink' if they are to read Charles Darwin's "Origins of the Species" and still believe what the bible tells us about our evolution? Has anyone seen recorded proof that Moses existed, did Noah really take all those animals for a jolly boat ride, is the world only 6000 years old, can we choose which of the stories in the bible are parables and which ones are meant to be believed? While some religions were developed in good faith and have benefitted our society in the past, it is pointless to continue with ideas that are now outdated, or no longer apply. Unfortunately, today's religious leaders want to maintain their positions in society and don't want to change or compromise their ideas, in case it ruins their career, and they must find a real job. I wouldn't want to offend anyone by listing the outdated beliefs, misconceptions and lies that these religious leaders continue to preach, but come on guys, just do some minor investigative work and check the background behind your chosen religion, and you will start to understand my doubts and concerns. If God had truly been responsible for any of the so-called sacred texts referenced by our holy leaders, why would they lose their integrity over time? The words may have been written with good intention, but they are the words of a human-being, rather than a God. In some cases, the texts have a more sinister intention based on ambition, power and control over the people, while being openly aggressive towards other beliefs and ideas. Some are purely based on estimations, lies and self-interest. At school I was taught about the importance of faith and what it meant to believe in something that you cannot see. Unfortunately, if you follow this principle into everyday life, you are going to come unstuck. There are many unscrupulous people in our society today, who will be only too happy to take advantage of you. While I don't believe in God's existence, I would be happy for you to argue your case as to why I should believe in him/her. However, if your facts and arguments prove to be full of holes, I will quickly doubt your credibility and demand to know why you are fucking with me. Just be honest with yourself, if someone told you that they were the son of God at the pub last night, you probably wouldn't believe them; so just because something was written down in an ancient text hundreds of years ago, doesn't necessarily mean that its true. Be careful, or you might as well believe in Scientology.

Starting to feel playful after a few pints, I lean in towards the table and remind Eileen that the U.K would still be a Roman Catholic country, if Henry 8th hadn't wanted to divorce Catherine of Aragon, to marry the fresh faced, possibly a virgin, Anne Boleyn, who may or may not have shagged her younger brother, George. Eileen carefully takes a sip of her white wine and peers up at me through her fringe.

"Are you familiar with Martin Luther's 95 Theses, Adam," she replies dryly.

I look at Bev who shrugs her shoulders and has another gulp of her wine. She didn't have anything to say on the 'subject of Religion', and her general demeanour indicated that she could take it or leave it, but her breasts did look marvellous, perched wonderfully beneath that tight white blouse.

It had been less than a week since meeting Bev and my outlook on life had already changed. I now wake each morning feeling more alive and seeing the world around me with a different pair of eyes. I feel stronger, lighter, happier, and more confident and self-assured and have taken to asking my Mum and Dad if they need anything doing. However, I also feel scared and vulnerable as I now have something to lose. While I am facing these contrasting emotions, Bev remains her bright and breezy self and doesn't appear to be going through the same type of inner conflict. She is consistently articulate, confident, witty, cheeky and marvellously bossy. I conclude from this, that whatever I am currently experiencing with my emotions, that Bev has been there already. Our relationship was mind-blowing for me, and while it obviously excited Bev, she seemed to be taking it in her stride. I wondered whether this meant that she had been in love before. We hadn't yet discussed our previous love interests, and while mine wouldn't produce an awfully long conversation, I am beginning to think that Bev has a story to tell.

During the following week, Bev worked part-time at the same Care Home as Eileen, while I was helping my dad again on the Window Round. I managed to call into the Home on a couple of occasions and helped with some heavy lifting. Then, after work, we would sit on a bench at Pennington Park and discuss some of our likes and dislikes, trying to ensure that we liked all the same things. I was keen to learn more about this fantastic woman and soaked up everything she said, like a giant sponge sucking her dry.

I soon found out that a couple of passing acquaintances of mine already knew Bev from school or college and the comments also tended to be positive, in her favour.

"How did you pull her?"

"You're punching above your weight."

"But she's really intelligent."

I'm not sure what these comments said about me, but I managed to take them all as compliments.

I wanted to be with Bev all the time and was conscious that I only had a limited time with her before she went to live in France, for almost 3 months. I was still going to the Brit to see my friends during the week, but my mind was totally consumed with thoughts of Bev, and I could think of little else.

Tony and I had arranged another double date on Saturday to celebrate my 20th birthday. It was a milestone that Bev had already passed in April and while this was only 5 months ago and one school year, it was evident that there was a difference in us in terms of maturity. Bev, however, didn't seem to mind that she had more life experience than me, in fact she seemed to consider it endearing. Was she trying to mould me into her perfect man? Did she just want to use me as a sex toy in the bedroom? I did hope so!

I didn't get to drive my dad's car very often as he tends to fret when my mum or I get within ten feet of the car keys. However, tonight he was relaxed after a couple of lunch time drinks and reluctantly handed over the keys. I went to pick up Bev and I met her parents for the first time. They were pleasant enough, but I got the feeling that Bev's mum already hated me. After a cracking birthday meal at an Italian restaurant in Boothstown, I drove the four of us back to Leigh where we settled at the Courts Hotel. Tony and Eileen seem to be easing into their relationship with an easy-going banter, but there is no high energy body language to speak of and I don't think they are falling in love. Tony has managed to bring Eileen out of her shell, but he has had to tone down his personality a bit and ultimately, he will need to find someone who is more outgoing and has more to say for herself. We see Mark and Chris in the Courts Hotel and they are going on to the Globe pub next, before heading back to the Britannia for last orders. Colin is in Bolton tonight meeting up with some old school friends of ours. It is a good night out in Bolton, and I promise to take Bev before we return to our university studies. It's this weekend that Paul and Teabag are in Brighton where they are planning to go to a new club that has opened on the beachfront, where Teabag's cousin is manning the door.

While the four of us are celebrating my 20th birthday, Prince Charles and Diana Princess of Wales are celebrating the birth of their second son, Prince Harry of Wales, and like me he will be a Virgo. That means he will be an ambitious, iron willed and a relentless perfectionist, who is self- aware, self- critical, independent and articulate. Well, Harry won't really need to be ambitious to make it in this world, but I wish him all the best of luck, because he will need most of these attributes if he is to survive his upbringing amongst our toxic Royal family. I'm sure his mother will try desperately to keep him on the straight and narrow but having a wet father like Charles, who plays polo badly and talks to plants, won't be much use to him. It is obvious to everyone with green eyes that the two of them aren't suited and while an age difference needn't be a major problem to a long and happy marriage, I think it will be in this case. He acts older than his years, while she possesses a childlike quality which is endearing but seems to annoy him. I think that he needs to find himself someone like Jane Austen who can organise his social events and prevent his life from getting too exciting, while she already seems to have a keen eye on her bodyguard. I do like Princess Diana, along with the Queen and Princess Anne, but I'm troubled by all the men in that mixed up family and there are too many hangers- on for my liking. In short, I think the whole bloody establishment desperately needs modernising. However, the government prefer to use them as another layer of establishment to keep us subservient, while occasionally attacking them to deflect attention away from their own misdemeanours.

The following Wednesday I take Bev along to Old Trafford to watch Man United's first European game of the season. It ends in a 3.0 victory over Raba Eto Gyor from Hungary. Bev seems to enjoy the game, making encouraging noises at the appropriate times and a few inappropriate comments about how fit Gary

Bailey's legs are. I just laugh and pretend not to feel at all jealous.

Later that week, a suicide bomber from the Islamic militant group Hezbollah attacks the U.S embassy in Beirut killing 24 people. Hezbollah means 'Party of God' and was the brainchild of Lebanese clerics who adopted the model set out by Ayatollah Khomeini after the Iranian Revolution in 1979. The group was motivated by the Israeli invasion of Lebanon in 1982 and is driven by its opposition to Israel and resistance to Western influence in the Middle East. They have promised not to allow a single American citizen to remain on Lebanese soil. It is becoming increasingly apparent that religious tensions are rising across Asia with the Mujahideen now prominent in Afghanistan, following the Soviet invasion in 1979 and continued U.S interference. The Mujahideen are Islamic guerrillas who engage in jihad, and they are attracting Muslim volunteers from other like-minded countries such as Saudi Arabia. An extremist named Osama bin Laden from the wealthy Saudi family, is known to be a major organiser and financier of an all-Arab Islamist group of foreign volunteers, funnelling money, arms and fighters into Afghanistan. It is concerning that the Cold War appears to be causing issues that are likely to come back and haunt us in the future.

Another Wednesday and we go to Wigan on the bus spending the day wandering about looking at the shops. I bought a couple of books, including Wuthering Heights by Emily Bronte while Bev bought some make-up and a red lipstick. We had a couple of drinks at the Swan and Railway pub near Wigan Pier but decided to get back to Leigh before the evenings drinking commenced. I've had a few good nights in Wigan, but you do have to have your wits about you, as it's not known as the Wild West for nothing. It's usually best to avoid eye contact in case you end up with a 'Glasgow Kiss' on your nose, and that's just from the girls. We got back to Leigh at about 7.30. It was another perfect day.

Manchester United drew with Liverpool 1-1 on Saturday and I make good on my promise by taking Bev to Bolton for a night on the town. A school friend of mine is playing a gig with his band in Bolton, and I had promised that I would go along to support him. They play standard Rock Music to a reasonable level, but I don't think that they will be making it big, any time soon. I speak to Michael at the interval and introduce him to Bev. He seems suitably impressed, especially when she speaks a little accented French. She could have been saying 'I'm just going for a dump' but in French it would still sound sexy. Michael is studying at Trinity and All Saints College in Leeds and will be going back to Leeds within the next couple of weeks. We enjoyed a pint of Timothy Taylors 'Landlord' and spoke about the crazy nights that we had spent drinking Coates's Triple Vintage cider at the Howcroft's Inn down the road, before heading off to a nightclub to try our luck with the ladies. Frank Hardcastle was the landlord of the Howcroft's back then and he would sometimes limit the consumption of this cider to people he didn't know, because 3 pints was enough for anyone. His wife had sadly passed away in 1980 and we heard on the grapevine that he had retired to Blackpool in 1983. Colin and I spent a lot of time with Michael in the 6th form and enjoyed many a good night out together, but it is getting harder to keep in touch with everyone, and I would be surprised if we are still in contact after beginning our careers.

Moving on, we see Mark in Yates' Wine Lodge drinking their famous 'Ozzy white' wine which is a lethal brew. He drinks 3 glasses while we are with him and then walks into the ladies' toilets by mistake. His friend Stephen is lying on his back in the middle of the pub, but no-one seems particularly concerned. I bump into a few other faces that I went to school with, and I feel proud to be with such an amazing vibrant young woman. We call in the fabulous 'Dog and Partridge' and visit 'Spencer's Bar' which is owned by 3 times World snooker champion John Spencer. We take a walk by 'Cinderella Rockefellers', which is on the corner of Bridge Street and St Georges Road and was a regular haunt of ours when I was out in Bolton with Colin and Michael. When I first walked into the club, I thought it was massive because I could see loads of people looking back at me from all corners of the room, only to realise that the walls were full of mirrors, and I was one of those people.

Finally, I take Bev to 'Ye Olde Man & Scythe' which is the oldest pub in Bolton and probably one of the oldest in the U.K. The oldest mention of its name is from a charter in 1251 when Henry 3rd, (son of King John of Magna Carta fame and nephew of King Richard the Lionheart) was King of England, Lord of Ireland, and Duke of Aquitaine. It's hard to imagine the history that has occurred while this pub has been standing and the stories it could tell of events taking place during the last 734 years. In 1651 the Earl of Derby was executed outside the pub (owned at the time by his family) for the part he played in the Bolton

Massacre of 1644 which took place during the English Civil War. Bolton, which was a strong Parliamentarian town was stormed and captured by Royalist forces and up to 1600 inhabitants of the town were slaughtered during and after the fighting. Only the vaulted cellar remains of the original structure, though some internal beams remain from when the pub was rebuilt in 1636. It is now a Grade 2 listed building. While I'm sure Bev is absolutely fascinated by my history lesson, she currently seems more interested in getting another glass of wine before last orders.

Whenever I stop to say hello to another old school friend she slips easily into the conversation and manages to cast her magical spell on everyone that she meets. It is a skill I would love to possess one day, and I hope that some of her aura will begin to rub off on me. Nothing phases Bev and she seems to thrive on new experiences or meeting new people. I can't get enough of her, and we haven't even had sex yet!

I couldn't have been any happier, if it wasn't for the small matter of her departure to France on the 30th of September, and so we try to see each other as often as possible. We spend hours walking hand in hand around Leigh Flash, past the golf course and up to the Bridgewater Canal, following the path back into town. I think back to when I was a boy walking a similar route with my friends, blissfully happy and without a care in the world and it's hard not to feel nostalgic.

On the 28th of September, the Miner's strike is ruled illegal as no National Ballot of NUM members had been held. The picket line violence has been getting worse and 6 deaths have been reported, with some miners being arrested and charged. Slowly, but surely, the tide has turned, and Margaret Thatcher has all but won the battle. Arthur Scargill is now being ridiculed by the press while the strength of the Trade Unions is crumbling and the close- knit communities of South Yorkshire are beginning to lose heart. In 1980, Margaret Thatcher was quoted as saying "The lady's not for turning". Well, she's turning now! With victory in her grasp, she is 'turning her back' on the communities of Yorkshire and Lancashire and consigning our working-class heroes to the shit heap of poverty, for the foreseeable future.

Good job Maggie, you truly are the UK's very own 'Wicked Witch of the South'.

I attempt to discuss the consequences of the Miners' strike with Bev, but her glazed eyes make it clear that she doesn't do politics. I wonder what part of the working classes Maggie will set her sights on next. There has always been a strong connection between Football and the mining communities in the North of England and many clubs have actively been supporting their local miners throughout the strike. Is it inconceivable that her next attack will be on Football itself?

Manchester United beat West Brom 2-1 away from home on Saturday and it was finally time for Bev and me to talk about the future. I hadn't wanted to rock the boat earlier than necessary, but Bev was leaving for France tomorrow and a discussion needed to take place. As usual, Bev was the better communicator and managed to allay my fears about our 11-week separation. She promised that her love for me was genuine and that she was 100% committed to our relationship, despite it now becoming a long- distance relationship. She was going to write to me every week to keep me updated about her life in France and to share with me her intimate thoughts and feelings. Most importantly, she was going to remain faithful and insisted that I could trust her. She had also written down the telephone number of her landlady in France and taught me how to ask for her politely in French. I brought up the subject of sex, explaining that I hadn't wanted to put pressure on her, knowing that she was about to leave the country. Bev smiled and thanked me for my patience and kindness but admitted that she too had been craving sex and had on occasions been ready to 'explode her juices'. I was happy with these comforting words and was now convinced that Bev was the woman I was going to spend the rest of my life with. I had the world in the palm of my hands and now felt that I could achieve anything.

The following day, I went with Bev's parents to see her off on to the train bound for London, which was the first part of her journey to Paris. Later that day Eileen ended her relationship with Tony with a brief telephone call. Beverley would be back in England on Saturday 15th December and so I had two and half months to think about all the lovely sex that we were going to enjoy. I just hoped that she would be gentle with me.

The year ahead was going to be important for my degree as my second- year exams would account for about 40% of my final qualification. I knew that I had to be responsible and get my head down and focus on the job in hand, despite the loss of Bev to another country. Hopefully, her absence would be a good thing and give me greater focus before her return at Christmas.

The university lads still have another week before returning to our studies, so we plan one final night out in Leigh to draw a line under a wonderful summer. I see that Paul has bought a new shirt for the occasion and question him about his trip to Brighton. While he is a little cagey about what they got up to, he said that the new club was amazing, and the atmosphere was electric. He obviously can't wait to go back, so he must have had a great time. Mark kicks off the evening as though he is on a mission, Colin is on top form with his one- liners, and Tony and Chris end up talking about important Rugby matters. I take in my surroundings and get absolutely smashed.

On Sunday, I pick up the copy of Wuthering Heights by Emily Bronte, that I bought in Wigan and wonder if Cathy and Heathcliff have anything in common with Adam and Bev. I do hope that the book remains true to that amazing song by Kate Bush, I hate it when books don't live up to their songs.

CHAPTER 5.
SALFORD

Sunday October 7th- October 19th, 1984.

I make my way back to Salford on Sunday evening and meet up with my 3 flat mates for the coming year. This year I will be living with Mark, Nick and Mike. I spent a lot of time at the flat last year visiting Mark and so I already know Nick and Mike. Trevor, who lived with them last year has moved out to live with his girlfriend, so I have taken his place. Once the four of us have unpacked our gear we make our way to the Church public house to catch up on the events of the summer break.

Nick is tall, skinny, and blonde, loves his football and supports his home team Sheffield United. He is easy going, friendly and quiet, unless he has been drinking, at which point he turns into Oliver Reed on crack. He is in love with a girl he sees at the Bingo in Sheffield, when he takes his Nan out on a Thursday, during the holidays. He hasn't spoken to her yet, but her name is Debbie, and she has a lovely laugh. He is studying Economics.

Mike is small but athletically built, comes from somewhere in Cheshire and is studying Mathematics.

He is a born-again Christian and rather eccentric but is also extremely likeable. He is giddy to see us all again, is very talkative and can't wait to hear all the details about my new girlfriend. He joins us at the pub even though he doesn't drink alcohol and has a coke. He is full of the joys of Christ tonight and doesn't stop laughing all evening. Mike is a true star and I love spending time with him because of his infectious positive energy.

Getting a place at Salford University was perfect for me as it is just up the East Lancashire Road from Leigh. It has a similar Industrial heritage to Leigh and allows me to pop back home whenever the mood takes me. I don't think I would have suited one of those posh Universities like Oxford or Cambridge, so I refused all their bribes and sweeteners to join them and remained close to my northern roots.

Salford, like Leigh, has a Rugby League team, which has won 6 Championships and 1 Challenge Cup, since its formation in 1873. Consequently, it has been a little more successful than Leigh, but its best years were during the 1930's, when it won 4 of its 7 major trophies. Alex Murphy was the Salford coach in 1978 in between playing for and managing Leigh and he was replaced by Kevin Ashcroft in 1980 who had already played for and managed Leigh. My Dad used to clean Kevin Ashcroft's windows on a fortnightly basis.

Salford also had a major cotton and silk spinning and weaving industry in the 19th and 20th centuries and became an important inland port on the Manchester ship canal from 1894. The opening of the Bridgewater Canal in 1761 improved the transport of fuel and raw materials, reducing the price of coal by about 50%. However, following the Great Depression of the 1920s and 1930s its industries declined to the point where Salford had some of the worst slums in the country. Due to the squalid conditions and the filth and the grime, many of its houses were infested with rats and in a terrible state of repair, with leaking roofs, broken flooring and rotten woodwork, all common features. Despite this, the working-class communities of Salford were made up of proud people who worked hard to keep their houses clean and respectable under the most adverse of conditions. Unfortunately, local mining in Salford had ended by 1939 while cotton spinning had ceased by 1971 and unemployment was high. Large areas of the city underwent development in the 1960s and 1970s and the Victorian era housing estates which had inspired the paintings of L.S Lowry and Tony Warren's Coronation Street were replaced by grim concrete tower blocks and austere architecture.

And it is one of those dirty grim concrete tower blocks named 'Larch Court' that the four of us now call home in 1984. Salford University owns flats in both Larch Court and Poplar Court and rents them out as student accommodation. They are unsightly monstrosities but are practical for students and comparatively cheap compared with other student accommodation. Consequently, we have become a part of Salford's obscene levels of deprivation and are distinctly aware of the high levels of local unemployment that has resulted in increased levels of gang crime, illegal drugs, and burglaries. Fortunately, the families of Larch and Poplar Court don't have much to worry about, because no-one here has 'a pot to piss in' and their worldly possessions aren't attracting the attention of any self -respecting burglars. We do have

3 small black and white portable televisions in our flat, but we manage to feel safe in our relative prosperity and sleep soundly in our beds at night.

If the people of Leigh wanted to know what its future holds, I would probably ask them to look at Salford now. However, while the boys of Eton, Harrow and other similar high- profile establishments, would be appalled by the state of Salford and catch the next helicopter home, Mark and I are reasonably comfortable in our surroundings. We are familiar with the locals that we live amongst, recognise the poverty in the city and feel at home with the pubs in the area. While the students of Salford complain about their treatment in the local pubs, Mark and I haven't had any such issues.

Both Karl Marx and Frederick Engels, spent some time in Salford studying the plight of the British working classes. In 1844 Engels described Salford as

"a very unhealthy, dirty and dilapidated district"

Unfortunately, for us, Salford has deteriorated since then.

On Monday morning my first letter arrives from France, it is pink and scented and has real French stamps and a French postmark. I've never had a letter from France before and am happier than a sandboy, a clam, a lark and Larry, all rolled into one. The letter talks about Bev's accommodation, the school and her pupils, but is mostly about what she is going to do to me when she returns from France. I walk into my first lecture this morning with an enormous erection and almost knock a couple of chairs over. Following my Contemporary History lecture, I catch up with my friend John and we exchange news. I met John on the first day of university last year when we both realised that we had just missed our first ever lecture. We then bonded during our second lecture, when he realised that sitting on the back row of the auditorium wasn't a good idea, because he was short sighted and couldn't see the white board at the front of the room. John is doing a similar course to me but chose the Politics option rather than Economics. He is a similar build to me and is tall with long unwashed black hair and a long, but not unattractive nose. He has a cheeky smile and a nervous laugh and is a good-looking guy. John comes from Wolverhampton but supports Leeds United, probably because they were the best football team in England when he was growing up. When he arrived at university, he had a girlfriend called Maja who was also from Wolverhampton. When she had been offered a place at Manchester, John managed to get into Salford, so that they could remain close. Unfortunately, they split up after a few months and she started to see someone else with an even bigger nose. He can appear very laid-back in his demeanour, but he is a worrier and can fuss over the smallest matters. This year, he will be living at Castle Irwell again with the same group of lads that he was with last year. Castle Irwell is the main student accommodation for Salford University and is less than a mile walk, to both the University and Larch Court. After our lectures, John goes to the library while I go to buy one of my course books from the book shop, before returning to Larch Court for tea.

Nick is already there with his friend Ian who is on the same Economics course. They met on the first day of university in similar circumstances to John and I and Ian also lives at Castle Irwell with the same group of friends that he shared with last year. Ian is from Liverpool and is a massive football fan, supporting Liverpool. To call him a typical 'scouser' would be underestimating Ian because you couldn't accuse him of being average. He is cleverer, funnier and cheekier than most scousers and is always laughing at my jokes, so he must have a fantastic sense of humour. Ian is a great organiser and runs the 'Social Sciences' football team and wants John and I to join him this year, as his centre half pairing. He usually plays in goal for the team but also fancies himself as a striker, in the same mould as Ian Rush. He isn't quick but he does have a good eye for a goal. Ian shares accommodation with Richard, who is the team's right back and Ron, who sometimes gets dragged out of bed to provide emergency left back cover for Pete, who is a 'ladies' man and doesn't always turn up on a Sunday morning.

After tea, Mark, Nick, Ian and I, go up to my room to play darts on an old Dartboard that I found in my dad's garage. Mike isn't playing tonight as he is hosting a Bible meeting in his room downstairs. By the look of some of the girls arriving at the flat to attend Mike's meeting, I think Mark and Nick are starting to feel more religiously inclined

The first week at university goes well with everyone quickly settling into the routine of Lectures, Tutorials, Library, Course work, Pub and Bed. It is on Friday that news starts to filter through of an assassination attempt on Margaret Thatcher and her cabinet at The Brighton Grand Hotel. A long delay time bomb has been planted by the IRA which has killed 5 people connected with the Conservative Party and injured 31. The bomb detonated at approximately 2.54

a.m. and brought down a chimney stack that crashed through the floors, fortunately, without causing the whole hotel to collapse. Apparently, Margaret Thatcher was still awake at the time of the blast and despite some damage to their bedroom, she and her husband Dennis escaped unhurt. By 4 a.m., and in true Margaret Thatcher style, she was giving an interview confirming that the Conference would be going ahead as planned.

While many people legitimately despise Margaret Thatcher, her speedy response to the bombing demonstrated once more, why she will probably go down as one of the greatest politicians and leaders of the 20th century. In many ways she reminds me of Winston Churchill, who was also a proud, arrogant, stubborn, single-minded politician who made a lot of mistakes. Like Thatcher, this often earned him a bad reputation amongst many of his colleagues. Fortunately for the UK, he was also a man who could get a job done at a time of crisis for the country. Both politicians possess a strength of purpose that made a huge difference when the people of the United Kingdom needed their leader to step up.

Yes, Margaret Thatcher is the Wicked Witch of the South, but today she is our Wicked Witch in the South.

My flat mates and I talk at length about the objectives of the IRA and the likely outcome of this blatant act of terrorism. A United Ireland? Emancipation for the Catholics? A united Ireland sounds reasonable, but many in the North consider themselves to be British and don't want the country to unite. As for whether the Irish Catholics have a legitimate grievance of discrimination against the British government and the Irish Unionists is now moot, as they have lost the moral high ground by resorting to murder. The resulting fallout from the explosion has allowed Margaret Thatcher to take control of the aftermath of the attack and won her universal admiration, while uniting the British people against terrorism. There were of course some people that spoke up against her.

Morrisey of my favourite band, the Smiths, joked -

"The only sorrow of the Brighton bombing is that Thatcher escaped unscathed".

A working men's club in South Yorkshire, angered by her treatment of the miners, asked for a whip round to pay for the bomber to have another go.

However, in the main, the British people viewed the bombing as an attack on their country, which has impacted badly on the Irish Catholic's grievances about the injustices they are facing in the North because of the British Government, and the Irish Protestant Unionists. The atrocities currently being committed by the UVF, and the UDA against the Irish Catholic civilians don't command the equivalent levels of news coverage that the biased BBC and British press devote to the IRA, and now this bias will only get worse.

The British people in the main would not be aware of the 1964 peaceful civil rights campaign in Northern Ireland, attempting to end the discrimination against the Catholics by the Protestant Unionist Government. They probably will not recall that it was 'a Reverend' a so called 'Holy man' who instigated and led loyalist opposition to the civil rights movement, vehemently opposing the policies of reform and reconciliation. They probably wouldn't realise that the IRA was inactive at this time and that a great opportunity existed to rid the country of its inequalities. In truth, they couldn't really have been expected to know, because while they would have heard plenty about the evils of South Africa's Apartheid system via 'BBC Newspeak', they weren't hearing anything about the evils of the Irish Apartheid system, much closer to home.

In April 1966, the Reverend founded the Ulster Constitution Defence Committee and its paramilitary wing, the Ulster Protestant Volunteers while at the same time, a loyalist paramilitary group calling itself the 'Ulster Volunteer Force' (UVF) emerged in the Shankill area of Belfast. The Reverend publicly thanked the UVF for taking part in a march organised on the 7th of April and then remained tight-lipped in May and June, when they petrol bombed Catholic homes, schools and businesses. The group later shot dead two Catholic civilians as they walked home, murders that are often seen as the first deaths of 'the Troubles' But who is this Reverend that seems to be dictating Religion and Politics in Northern Ireland? How does he manage to juggle Jesus Christ and murder? Is he not the country's greatest reason, for introducing secularism into Northern Ireland?

On 6th June 1966, the Reverend Ian Paisley led a march through a Catholic neighbourhood carrying placards with anti-Catholic slogans inciting violence. However, the Royal Ulster Constabulary (RUC) come down on the side of the marching Protestants when trouble breaks out. Then, on 30th November 1968, the Reverend arrived in Armagh, hours before a Catholic civil rights march, along with men armed with nail studded cudgels in order to prevent the peaceful march. Again, the RUC intervenes, only to side once more with the Protestants, by preventing the march.

The civil rights campaign culminated in August 1969 with further attacks on it by Loyalists and the Police who invaded Catholic neighbourhoods and burned down homes and businesses. This led to the deployment of British troops and marked the beginning of the Troubles and a state of 'perpetual war', which many in the UK mistakenly blame on the IRA.

To make matters worse, the irreverent reverend, is still getting plenty of air- time on the BBC in 1984, using the same disgusting rhetoric to promote his evil views to the nation. Many of my friends cannot understand why I get so worked up when I see this evil bastard on T.V. I am not a fan of Margaret Thatcher, but this man is the Devil and I really do hate him. I strongly believe that the Brighton Bombing would not have happened if this man had kept his evil thoughts to himself and I haven't even touched on his campaign against the homosexuals of Northern Ireland.

'Save Ulster from Sodomy'.

Sadly, the Brighton bombing did happen, and Margaret Thatcher will probably get into power for a third time in 1987, as a result of her handling of the aftermath, despite yet another major industry in the North being confined to Coal Dust.

What isn't yet clear, is what she has planned for us all after 1987, at which point her ego will be so huge that she will consider herself unstoppable, even within her own party.

Maybe she will realise that it is now time to do something to reverse the current trend in the North of England by introducing some form of investment, that will enable us to bounce back from the many knocks we have had to deal with during the 20th century. A 'Northern Powerhouse' perhaps, to kickstart our economy and put it on an even footing with our distinguished Southern landlords. Yes, maybe Maggie will sit down with her cabinet to consider how best to approach the ever- increasing North/South divide, but I wouldn't count on it.

More likely, however, is that Northern folk will continue to be downtrodden and ignored, unless they are required once more for 'cannon fodder'. Sartre once said that 'when the rich wage war, it's the poor who die'. Unfortunately, if there is another war that requires the bravery of those hard- working communities that provided the men required to fight two world wars, those in charge of recruitment are likely to find that they no longer exist.

But it's not all bad news, in 1984 there are always opportunities for a handful of working-class northerners, possessing the necessary skills, to make it successful in the UK, but you might need to play football, sing a few songs or make everyone laugh. Alternatively, you could try it the hard way via the education system, but at some point, you will need to learn how to shaft your fellow man, if you are to be successful. Only when you have proven your lack of morals will you finally be able to take your place with the elite at the top table, but even then, they will secretly despise you for not being quite 'the right sort'. The boys from Eton and Harrow will continue to hold all the power as they have done throughout the centuries, while continuing to have a good laugh at our expense. It doesn't really matter what career you choose; the bastards will still be looking down at you from the top of their shit pile and we will happily continue donning our flat caps, taking the whippet for a walk and gratefully accepting our lot.

Mark and I go to watch Man United beat West Ham United 5-1 on Saturday and I play my first game of football for the Social Sciences team on Sunday. We are 2-0 down after 5 minutes due to the opposition team's very speedy centre forward running through the heart of our defence to score twice. This meant trouble for the new centre half pairing of Adam and John, who needed to find a solution quickly. Consequently, we made an adjustment whereby John would mark him closely to put him off his stride while I would hang back a little and then nail him while he was off balance. He still got himself a hat-trick in our 7-4 defeat, but we considered this a victory and immediately set off to the Church pub to celebrate.

A second letter arrived from Bev on Monday which was still sexy but also a little sad. She was feeling understandably lonely living alone in a foreign country with a lot of responsibilities in her new teaching role. However, having known Bev now for almost 5 weeks, I am confident that she will soon begin to make friends and successfully settle down in France. I go to the telephone box in the shopping arcade after 6 o'clock and give her a call to cheer her up. She is pleased to hear from me, and we have a chat about how we are getting on in our respective worlds. The call is brief due to a lack of coins, but I return to the flat feeling a little happier and I'm sure that Bev will feel the same.

Mark and I go to the Flemish Weaver on Wednesday to watch England beat Finland 5-0 in their first World Cup Qualifier for the 1986 World Cup. We have a quiet one because we have a big session planned for Saturday in Salford. We discuss our contrasting courses, and while Mark has a lot more lectures, I need to spend more time in the library. I don't mind being in the library as it allows me to discuss and exchange essays written with my colleagues, so that we can broaden our thoughts and perspectives on a subject. This becomes increasingly necessary when the books required for study are never available in the library. It is good to share ideas with others because not everyone will have the same opinions on important matters. I'm sure there will be people somewhere who have a different view of Margaret Thatcher or Jane Austen, because we can't all be right.

It is stimulating talking to Mark over a few beers because he has a wide spread of knowledge on most subjects and is easy to talk to. We talk about Music, Sport, Politics, Religion, and Philosophy and while our views aren't always aligned, we do agree that we are living in a 'crazy mixed- up world'. We discuss what we want out of our lives and Mark seems to have a clearer vision than I do. High on his priority list is the love of a good woman, a couple of kids and maybe a cat and a dog. His career is easier to choose because of his interest in Electrical Engineering but he seems to favour a simple life rather than an ambitious one. Music and Sport will always remain important to him, and he seems to have no desire to abandon his Leigh roots, so I don't think that he will end up moving abroad, chasing the money. His family originates from Ireland, and he often wears his green Rugby Union top with great pride and talks fondly of his Irish relatives but I'm not sure whether he would ever re-locate there. He is already planning to purchase a motor bike rather than a car when his career kicks off, so that will further cement his strong working- class image. While Mark is highly intelligent, he is introverted and isn't always comfortable talking to certain types of people. Like me, he also has some issues with authority, especially when it is clear, that said authority is being abused.

The following day Mark is stopped by a Policeman and asked to stand in a 'line out' in 'Room 101' of the police station, because the accused is dressed in a similar working- class fashion. I couldn't help but laugh when Mark told me that the victim picked him out of the line up as the perpetrator of the crime. 'Fucking typical,' said Mark.

Mark and I don't dress like students and tend to blend in with the locals. I wear old shirts and jeans that I no longer use for 'going out', while Mark wears the same jeans and tee shirts, that he would for going out in Leigh. Of all the close friends I have made at university, only John dresses and acts like a student. Students tend to hate the 'uniforms' of their elders yet all wear the same black clothing and act as though they are political anarchists. Most of them come from wealthy backgrounds and will be just like their parents in 10 years' time, rather than striving to improve the world. I sometimes wonder how they view Mark and I, but at least we don't get beaten up by the locals, who can spot most students a mile away.

CHAPTER 6.
LOSING FOCUS.
20th October – 15th December 1984.

At 7 o'clock on Saturday evening Mark, Nick and I head for the Lower Broughton area of Salford to meet up with Ian, Richard, Ron and John to celebrate the start of the new academic year. Shelagh Delaney was born in Broughton in 1938 and wrote 'A Taste of Honey' when she was only 19. The play was set in Salford in the 1950's and attempts to address issues of class, race, sexual orientation and gender that she thought wasn't being represented by the mainstream media. While London had its angry young men such as John Osborne and Kingsley Amis, whose backgrounds didn't suggest that they had much to be angry about, Shelagh Delaney came from a poor working-class background and knew what she was complaining about. Morrisey's' favourite actress, 'Rita Tushingham', starred as 'Jo', in the 1961 film version of the play, in which she performed the first ever interracial kiss on screen, became a single mother at 18 and shared a flat with a homosexual man. It is quite disturbing that social injustices have been wrote about and highlighted in many different forms throughout the centuries, yet the same inequalities still exist in 1984. Interestingly, punk poet, John Cooper Clarke and Mark E Smith from music band, 'the Fall' are also from the Broughton area of Salford.

Pleasingly, Manchester United have beaten Spurs 1-0 today and Mark and I are keen to get the party started. We all meet up at the 'Griffin' which is a large pub on the corner of Lower Broughton Road. Mark and I used to meet here every Wednesday night in our first year at university when I was living in a large private house, about a 5 minute- walk away. My landlady rented four of her rooms out to Salford University students, but student related shenanigans weren't part of the tenancy agreement. If she heard loud voices or heavy footsteps on the landing, she would bellow upstairs, telling everyone to be quiet. It was expensive and wasn't an enjoyable place to live, but it helped me to remain focused during my first year at university. The house over-looked the 'Cliff' which is Manchester United's training ground, and when I was walking into the University in a morning, I would often see the players arriving for training in their expensive cars. The players I would recognise behind the wheel of their cars were Bryan Robson, Norman Whiteside, Paul McGrath and Jesper Olsen, all arriving at the facility, ready to put in the hard work, before Mark and I would watch them strut their stuff on the pitch on Saturday. It felt surreal living so close to the training ground of the team I had supported all my life, and I will always cherish that memory.

Mark and I both had Wednesday afternoons off during our first year at university, so we would often meet up after lunch, have some tea at my place and then go to the Griffin for a few pints, while watching the highlights of whatever football games had taken place that evening. There was a man, probably in his mid-fifties that used to come into the pub at last orders every Wednesday and order 4 and half pints of Lager. As soon as the bell for last orders rang, he appeared, put in his order, and took his seat at a table, and lined up his drinks. He would then stare into space without a single drop touching his lips, until he suddenly came to life, gulped down a pint and half of Lager before returning to his stare. This process would be repeated twice more before he stood up, put his coat on and left the pub. Mark and I never spoke to the man as he didn't appear to be the approachable type, but we would have loved to know his story. Had he told his wife that he was going out for a quick walk, was there a dog tied up outside, I suppose we will never know.

Ian bought the first round of drinks which included a double vodka and coke for Ron, who doesn't usually drink. When Ron knocked back the drink quickly, I was a little concerned, but assumed that he knew what he was doing. There were 7 of us out tonight and Nick happened to comment that it was like a scene from Auf Weidersen Pet, a television programme that all of us are big fans of. Consequently, the next half hour was taken up by discussing who was going to represent each of the characters, for the remainder of the evening. Ian became Dennis because he was the oldest and most sensible of the group. He was briefly considered for the role of Moxy because of his Liverpudlian background, but this went to Richard who comes from Oldham, has red hair and looks a bit like a Moxy. Nick became Oz because of his height and his crazy tendency to walk over parked cars when drunk. Mark was a shoe in for Bomber because of his build, while John became Barry due to his Wolverhampton background. I became Wayne because of my hairstyle and hips and because I was the only one with a girlfriend, at the current time. We had an issue with Ron who is tall, thin and black, so he became Neville by default. Unfortunately, Neville's evening was cut short after 3 double vodkas, when Ron was sick as a dog and had to go home. The remaining 6 of us made our way up to the Priory pub, which is opposite the Cliff Training Ground. Inside, Paul McGrath and Norman Whiteside were having a quiet pint at the bar. They stood chatting away with no-one bothering them for almost an hour and could have been a plumber and an electrician having a couple of well- earned pints on a Saturday, rather than 2 footballers playing for one of the biggest clubs in the world.

After another 3 pints, Dennis insisted that we carry on up the hill to the 'Star', which had a one- armed landlord they named Arthur. This would be the first visit to the Star for Bomber, Barry and Wayne, but we admired the lack of ambience, so it wouldn't be the last time we saw Arthur and his pub. We ended up playing a few games of Killer on the pool table in the back room of the pub and managed another 3 pints before heading back down Lower Broughton Road. By this point we were steaming drunk, and Oz did his customary car walking stunt, while the rest of us pretended that we didn't know him. I really do think that he needs to stop drinking.

We arrived at the Union Bar just after 10 o'clock and carried on drinking until the early hours of the morning. As we fell into our beds later that night,

Ron was getting up to catch the 5 o'clock train back to Leeds, to have Sunday lunch with his parents. I don't think he will be drinking again, any time soon.

Thankfully, we didn't have a football game on the Sunday morning, so I finished reading Wuthering Heights. I was surprised at how gritty the writing was and enjoyed the book even more than Jane Eyre, a book that I had previously enjoyed, by her sister Charlotte. I wondered if Jane Austen might have had something more interesting to write about, if she had been for a couple of bracing walks across the Yorkshire Moors.

The night out in Salford was supposed to kickstart the new academic year, but it did the opposite for me, as I became side-tracked by thoughts of Bev. A couple more letters had arrived from France and Bev now seemed to be finding her feet and had begun socialising with friends in and around Paris. Her teaching role was going well, and she was popular with the teachers and the students. I am extremely proud of what she is achieving; but I can't help wishing that she were missing me more than it appeared in her latest correspondence. I have a photograph of Bev pinned on the wall next to my bed and can spend hours looking at it, while listening to music. In the photograph, Bev is smiling, and has her hair in a ponytail. She is wearing a blue and white armless tee-shirt and a pair of white shorts, which show off her beautiful long legs.

Manchester United lose to Everton twice in the space of 4 days, including a 5-0 hammering at Goodison Park on the same day that Ozzy Osbourne's wife, Sharon, gives birth to their third child. They decide to call her Kelly. The Social Sciences team do a little better than Manchester United with a win and a draw in their next 2 games. Following both matches we have a few drinks in the Church pub and the lack of focus on my work starts to become a cause for concern, as I fall behind with Essays and Tutorials. Mark also seems to be struggling to settle down and he attends a couple of concerts in Manchester, during the week. One night, I was sitting in the kitchen talking to Nick, and we heard someone running towards the flat. It was Mark and he seemed agitated. He was convinced that a large fish had been chasing him and was probably outside waiting for him. I looked around outside, but I couldn't see man or fish on the landing or near the lifts, so we did our best to calm him down. Once he was settled, he made himself a big plate of chips and went up to bed. I checked on him the following morning and found him fast asleep, lying on his back, with an untouched plate of chips still sat on his chest. We decide that we will abstain from drinking for the next four weeks.

With that agreed, I manage to spend more time in the library and pick up momentum with my course work. I use the incentive of December being party month at the university and Bev's return to England, to get myself back on track. I put in a couple of all-nighters to write my essays, while the house is quiet and everyone else is asleep. I complete my tutorials at the library without any distractions and try to avoid the tv during the evenings. The month of November goes well, and I am caught up with my studies again, in a little over 2 weeks.

Manchester United also have a good start to the month with victories over Arsenal (4-2), Leicester City (3-2) and Luton Town (2-0) in the League. They beat P.S.V. Eindhoven 1-0 in the Cup Winners Cup to qualify for the last 16 of the competition. The England football team also manage to surprise us all with an 8-0 away victory in Turkey, with the help of a Bryan Robson hat-trick.

We treat ourselves by watching Top of the Pops on Thursday and see Slade performing 'All join hand's' and Alvin Stardust singing 'I won't run away', which feels like a blast from the past, for those of us that used to enjoy the 'Glam Rock era' of the early 1970's. There is also a song by Jim Diamond called 'I should've known better' which is a cracker and an embarrassing appearance by a group named Matt Bianco. Mark likes to watch Saturday Superstore at the weekend because he is in love with blond 'posh bird' Sarah Greene, who used to present 'Blue Peter'. Apparently, someone rang the show to call the group 'a bunch of wankers' and I can now see that he may have had a point. I decide to give Bev another call and pop down to the telephone box in the precinct, to let her know what we've just been watching, and she is delighted to hear from me. An increase in post from France is also encouraging and it is apparent that Bev is becoming increasingly excited about her return to England next month.

By the 28th of November, I am satisfied that I am back on track with my work, and I can start to look forward to the Christmas Break and seeing Bev. That night Mark and I go to watch Man United in the first leg of the last 16 tie of the Cup Winners Cup, against Dundee United. The game ends in an exciting 2-2 draw with both teams playing exceptionally well. We retire to the Flemish Weaver after the match and decide to end our 'dry November' a few days early. This seems like a bad idea when two dozen Scottish football fans celebrating Dundee United's draw with Man United, turn up at the pub. However, rather than this being a potential for violence and mayhem, the guys are so good natured and full of light-hearted humour that Mark and I end up celebrating with them. The beer flows, the whiskey is quaffed, and a great night is had by all. At the end of the day, a draw is a draw and Man United are more than capable of going to Dundee and winning the return leg. That said, I am impressed by the current state of football in the Scottish League where the dominance of Rangers and Celtic is currently being challenged by the likes of Dundee United and Aberdeen. Aberdeen won the European Cup Winners Cup and European Super Cup in 1983 followed by the Scottish League and Cup double in the 1983-84 season, so I'm keeping my eye on their Manager Alex Ferguson, who just might be the man to take over at Old Trafford and knock Liverpool off their fucking perch. The bad head in the morning is well worth it following such a terrific night with the boys from Dundee.

December arrives on Saturday and Man United beat Norwich 2-0 in a league game at Old Trafford, but I am at the flat finishing off another essay, before the start of party week. I play for the Social Sciences team on Sunday, but we lose 5-2 as a result of a sloppy display, by our midfield diamond. On the way back to the flat I treat myself to a copy of the News of the World which my parents used to get in the 1970s. It has now been transformed into a tabloid but is still owned by Rupert Murdoch and remains focused on celebrity gossip and sex scandals. It is the Sunday equivalent to the Sun newspaper and is a great distraction when your mind has been focused on academic pursuits during the week, but it is third rate journalism, and the stories are laughable. My parents used to have the Daily Mirror delivered during the week which was good for sport and is a staunch supporter of the Labour party. A Czechoslovakian guy known as Robert Maxwell bought the Mirror Group Newspaper group for £113 million in July this year and has pledged to challenge the Sun to become Britain's top selling newspaper. He has done very well for himself because he was born into poverty in 1923 but now lives a flamboyant lifestyle, flying around in his helicopter and sailing in his yacht, the Lady Ghislaine, named after his daughter. Mirror journalist Joe Haines has claimed that Maxwell is a crook and a liar and can prove it, but I can't believe that the purchase of the Mirror Group would have been allowed in the U.K if this was the case. What will he be accusing Maxwell of next? Child sex trafficking!!!

The following Wednesday is Rock night, and it is the last one of the academic- year. The attendance is excellent, although 90% of attendees are lads wearing denim or leather jackets, sporting long greasy hair and faded denim jeans with badges stitched or ironed on to them. There are a handful of girls, that all look remarkably like the boys, apart from having cleaner hair and less spots. One of those girls is a Janice Joplin lookalike, Anna, who comes over to talk to us about her boyfriend, Keith, who happens to be studying Medicine at Durham University. It's a strange topic to choose because it is obvious that she has the hots for Mark and wants to find out more about him. She has the quirky mind of a Scientist, and her conversation is difficult to follow, but she is funny and makes us laugh. When 'the Chain' by Fleetwood Mac is played, she grabs hold of my arm and drags me onto the dance floor. Somewhat surprised, I ask Anna why she didn't ask Mark to dance with her.

'Oh, I couldn't do that', she says, 'I couldn't trust myself'

'And what makes you think you can trust yourself with me', I say, raising my eyebrows suggestively?

Anna starts to laugh. 'Oh, you are funny', she says.

'Thanks', I say, 'I surprise myself, sometimes.

The song ends with the 'Grand Prix' introduction music from the television programme, and I go to the bar to get the three of us another drink. I might even get myself a vodka chaser. Roy is standing by the bar with only an inch of his beer left in his pint glass, so I ask him he wants another.

'No thanks Adam', he says sadly, 'I've already had my safe three'.

Roy has long brown hair and reminds me of Neil from the 'Young Ones'. He plays for the Social Sciences team on the left wing and once had trials for Blackburn Rovers. I'm not sure what he has had trials for, because having seen him play, it couldn't have been for football.

Mark and I have similar tastes in Rock music with Black Sabbath, AC/DC, Rainbow and Motorhead being amongst our favourite heavy rock bands, but we also like the punk rock bands, like the Stranglers, Buzzcocks and the Sex Pistols. However, at the age of 14, we needed to pick a side and most of our social group favoured heavy rock and hated punk, so we pretended that we felt the same way. In addition to this white lie, Mark and I also had a secret that would have blown our credibility out of the water, if anyone else would have found out. During a conversation with Mark while drinking one of my dad's Party 7's at Christmas, we admitted to quite liking the songs of Abba. To be perfectly honest, I can't understand how anyone could dislike the wonderful tunes that Benny and Bjorn composed between 1974 and 1983, but I wasn't going to openly admit that in 1979. At about this time, we would attend the weekly school disco at our old Junior school, where the D.J would play 4 pop songs, to which the girls danced round their handbags, 2 heavy rock songs, to which my group of friends would shake their heads to and then 2 punk songs, which another group of lads would jump up and down to. There was always an underlying tension between the punks and the rockers, but nothing ever happened.

The Rock night felt nostalgic for me, listening to some of the bands that I hadn't heard for many years, but I thoroughly enjoyed the evening, and Mark and I had a good laugh. Anna stayed chatting with us for about an hour by which time we had safely concluded that she was a lovely and intelligent young woman but quite clearly as mad as a box of frogs.

They played a couple of Rainbow tunes from the album 'Down to Earth' which I bought in clear vinyl in 1979. 'All Night Long' was the opening song on side 1 of the album and 'Since you've been gone' was the opening song to side 2.

While my musical tastes, have expanded into other areas, I'm sure that Mark has already found his niche, and will remain a steadfast heavy rocker for the rest of his life. Our conversations during the evening are also nostalgic as we think about the concerts we attended as young teenagers and the bars we would try to get into in Manchester. At that time, we would often catch a bus into Manchester or Bolton at the weekend and spend most of the day looking around record shops and trying to build up the confidence to talk to any girls we would come across. As I have previously alluded to, these were difficult days for me and having a friend like Mark made them bearable. As we talk of that phase of our lives, I can now look back at those times with happier memories than I had while living them. In some ways it feels like Mark is still living those years, which is fine, if he is happy, and I think that he is. I suppose I could just ask him if he is happy and tell him how miserable I had felt at the time, but that would just be too weird.

And then came the biggest night of the term. Saturday night is Christmas party night and the disco at Castle Irwell is packed with celebrating students looking forward to the end of the academic year. All the guys are up for a great night, the drinking starts early, and the music, for once, is fantastic. As the atmosphere builds, the vodka shots are lined up next to the beers, the dance moves begin take shape and I meet a cute girl.

This certainly wasn't my intention when the night had begun, but mixing my drinks had made me vulnerable, and I was soon in her room at Castle Irwell, semi-clothed and snogging her pretty face off. I was completely lost in the moment, Bev was effectively seven days away, in another country, and the lower part of my brain was saying 'get in there, lad'. Her name is Caroline, she comes from Glasgow, and she has just come out of a long- term relationship. As I gazed down at her perky breasts and black g-string knickers, she asked me if I fancied some coke.

"No fanks", I struggle to say, with my tongue busy licking the rim of her belly button.   "l will juss tick wiv the voddy for now."

She laughed, and said she was talking about cocaine.

I have always been anti -drugs and the question stopped my tongue in its slippery tracks. I thought that drugs were unpredictable and dangerous but knew this sounded hypocritical, especially considering the amount I'd had to drink tonight.

"Are you ok, she said?"

"I think so", I say, suddenly realising how difficult it was to concentrate with a hard on.

"I should probably go".

"What, to the toilet?" she said, sounding confused.

"No, look I'm sorry, I haven't been honest with you."

"What about", she asks.

"I have a girlfriend who has been in France for the past few months and is due back next week."

"Oh right", said Caroline, "Is that an issue then?"

"Isn't it for you?"

"Not really, I just fancied a shag and a bit of coke on a Saturday night".

"Well, that's also a bit of a problem for me, I don't do drugs".

"And do you shag?"

"Well, not very often, I mean, yes, but I don't want to cheat on her."

"I see", said Caroline, now sounding posher than I'd remembered her 5 minutes ago. "And don't you think that ship has already left the harbour, considering your dick is currently pressing itself against my inner thigh?"

I was starting to sweat and was craving an end to my torment, so I eased off the bed and started to look for my clothes.

"Sorry", I said again, "I really am."

"Don't worry about it" said Caroline, lighting up a cigarette and beginning to enjoy my discomfort.

"I've got my coke and there's a vibrator in there", she said, pointing to the drawer. "Would you like to see it, it's huge?"

I thank her for being so understanding, but she is now starting to piss me right off. I leave the room and close the door behind me but can hear the sound of laughter coming from inside.

On my walk back to Larch Court at 3.00 a.m. I meet John walking in the opposite direction. John had hooked up with a 'red head' from Larch Court and was making his way back to Castle Irwell as I was doing the reverse. He found the turn of events quite funny, but I was already beginning to wonder what had possessed me to get myself into such a position, so easily.

What I wasn't aware of at this point was the tragedy that had occurred that night in Leigh. While I was almost succumbing to temptation in a Castle Irwell bedroom in Salford, a 14-year-old girl called Lisa Hession was being viciously attacked, while walking home from a party in Leigh and the police are now searching for her killer. A man walking his dog had found Lisa in a ginnel close to her home on Bonnywell Road, shortly before Midnight on Saturday December 8th. Mark and I were in complete shock when we found out what had happened. It is hard to imagine that such a violent act has taken place in our hometown where family values and community are so important. We can only hope that the person or persons responsible are caught quickly and made to pay for their evil crime.

The following day, Ian and Richard joined us at Larch Court for Christmas Dinner. Mark was at another concert and wouldn't be back until Midnight, so we were planning on eating as soon as he got home. I got a bit of stick from the Castle Irwell guys who had seen me sneak off with Caroline on the previous Saturday, but I smiled and said nothing. I was angry with myself for what I had done, but relieved that I hadn't taken things further. I had got over the embarrassment of my early exit from Caroline's room and had started to see the funny side of the whole debacle. As per usual, I said very little about what had happened and kept the details of the night's events to myself, but I'm sure that I will tell Mark at some point.

Mark was my only confidante when I lost my virginity at 14, although I did come close to telling my cousin Damian. I was worried about possible repercussions and was having nightmares about Mandy turning up at our house with a pram. I didn't even talk about the girl at the party when I was 18, when it might have seemed normal for a lad of my age to brag about his encounter with an experienced older woman

I'm even worse with my parents. There have been many occasions in my life where it should have been second nature to talk to them about something that I was excited about or something that was troubling me. Whether it was about bullying, getting into trouble with a teacher, falling off my bike, having a fight or liking a girl, I found it easier to say nothing.

Yes, I've always been secretive, but I'm not sure why. Maybe it's because I'm an only child without a sibling to share my thoughts with, or maybe it's a generational thing, with lads in particular feeling as though they need to act cool or shoulder their burdens, by just getting on with everything that life throws at them. It isn't something that I think I should be proud of, and I can think of many reasons why it's probably not healthy, but it is one of the aspects of my personality that I would like to change.

On Marks return to the flat we tucked into our Christmas Dinner and applauded ourselves afterwards, for a job well done. That evening Man United beat Dundee United 3-2 to progress through to the Quarter Finals of the Cup Winners Cup, so it was a successful night all round. I spent the next couple of days finishing off course work, and finally the term was over, and the Christmas break had arrived. Mark and I stayed over until Saturday morning and went to watch Man United beat QPR 3-0 before returning home to Leigh. I arrived home feeling excited at the prospect of seeing Bev again after 11 weeks apart, but also a little nervous about whether the chemistry would still be as strong.

Before meeting up with Bev later I had some time for reflection. I had handled our time apart badly and the term was an erratic one that lacked focus, compared with my first year at university. I know that I need to improve my attitude if I am to be successful in my 2nd year exams and have some growing up to do. However, what bothered me the most, was my behaviour last Saturday when my fidelity crumbled under the slightest of pressure. From now on, it is important that I follow a structure in my life by which I can live my 'best life' where my actions reflect my individual outlook. Consequently, I need to avoid similar circumstances in the future or give up drinking. Yeah right!

CHAPTER 7

CHRISTMAS CHEER.
December15th 1984- January13th 1985.

I meet up with Bev at 8 o'clock at the Courts Hotel, and as she enters the pub, she looks amazing. She totters over to me in her high heels wearing a big smile on her face, and with her arms open wide embraces me and then kisses me passionately. It was only one kiss, but it made up for all those kisses I'd missed out on, during the previous 11 weeks. I could hear a group of girls grumbling about such a public show of affection, but as Gary Glitter's 'Another rock and roll Christmas' played on the jukebox, I couldn't give a flying fuck.

Later that night we bumped into Bev's friend Scarlett in Reubens nightclub. She was with a married man called Pete who had two young children and a wife that didn't understand him. Scarlett was in an animated state of excitement as she told her sordid tale to Bev. I wondered about what kind of influence her behaviour might have on my girlfriend.

The following day, we met up with Tony and his new girlfriend Susan who is a couple of years younger than us, but very lively and a lot of fun. Tony is clearly enamoured with Susan, but she looks like she could be a bit of a minx. I like her very much and she gets on remarkably well with Bev. Tony has been working now for 18 months and is maturing at a faster rate than the university lads, as his responsibilities at the bank increase. He is already talking the Bank and the Industry lingo and things that would have made him laugh 12 months ago, are no longer funny. He is now living the capitalists dream and I wish him all the best of luck with his ambitions. I briefly wonder whether I will lose my sarcastic attitude about the evils of the corporate world, but I'm not going to worry about that just yet. My issue is bound to come with authority, especially when I become exposed to those power- hungry individuals, who like to throw their weight about, and act like a bunch of blood sucking pricks. Oh yes, my friends, don't think I haven't noticed you. Fortunately, my mood lightens after a few drinks and the four of us have a lovely evening.

I watch the Sports Personality of the year awards on tv, and it is no surprise that Torvill and Dean win the award for 1984, following their heroics in Sarajevo at the Winter Olympics, when they won the figure skating Gold Medal. They received twelve perfect 6.0's and six 5.9's at the event after skating to Maurice Ravel's 'Bolero' and were watched by a British Television audience of more than 24 million people. Middle distance runner, Sebastian Coe, came second having already won the competition in 1979 and snooker Champion Steve Davis came third.

Sebastian Coe won another gold medal for the 1500m at this year's Olympic Games in Los Angeles following his gold in Moscow four years ago. Daley

Thompson also repeated his gold medal heroics in the Decathlon while Tessa Sanderson won her first Gold for the Javelin Throw, beating her British rival Fatima Whitbread into third place. Malcolm Cooper won a gold medal for small bore rifle shooting while the men's Coxed fours of Richard Budgett, Martin Cross, Adrian Ellison, Andy Holmes and the young Steve Redgrave won Rowing gold. The British team won a total of 37 medals this year, including 5 golds, which was our best total medal haul since 1920.

John Currie and Robin Cousins have previously won the Sports Personality of the year award following figure skating gold medals at the Winter Olympics. However, only Bobby Moore has won the competition as a footballer, which is surprising for a football mad country, but probably reflects our lack of success on the international arena.

My next night out with Bev in Leigh is Christmas Eve and she invites an old school friend to join us, called Kate. Kate didn't go to university and has been working down south as a journalist for a couple of years. I have asked Colin to join us, and he is going to be my wingman for the evening. Kate is good-natured and easy to talk to and tells us what it is like living in London with all its bars, theatres and restaurants. She is obviously living a wonderful-life, and it seems unlikely that she will be returning to Leigh, any time soon. As for romance, there is no-one special, and neither Ian nor Kate, appear to be showing any signs of romantic feelings for one another tonight. The night ends with vodka shots and while Bev is a bit of a lightweight, it looks as though Kate might be a party animal. It is another enjoyable evening, and we all get on tremendously well. Tonight, I am stopping over at Bev's parents' house and so we part company with Colin and Kate at about 11.30 and go our separate ways. When we arrive at the house Bev's parents are still up, so I don't anticipate any sneaky bedroom action tonight. As expected, I am to be packed away in the spare room. However, 5 minutes later Bev appears in my room needing her dress unzipping at the back. As I carefully pull the zip downwards, towards her pert little bottom, I slide my finger down her spine, and she quivers with pleasure. Then, as I tenderly kiss the nape of her neck, Bev's mother appears at the door of the bedroom and the excitement is over for the night.

Christmas Day and Boxing Day are to be spent with the family, but Bev and I do meet up on Thursday to exchange gifts. The television has been appalling over the Christmas period with Jim'll Fix it, a film called 'One of our Dinosaurs is Missing', a repeated Only Fools and Horses classic and Val Doonican on his rocking chair, being the highlights for Christmas Eve. I can't watch Jimmy Saville on tv as he has given me the creeps since I was a small child, and I wouldn't let him 'fix a shelf' in our house. On Christmas Day we have the Queen's Speech at 3 o'clock followed by a choice of 'Mary Poppins' or 'The Man with the Golden Gun' as the seasons 'not so latest' blockbuster movies. The hilarious Les Dawson does his best to liven up 'Blankety-Blank' in the evening, followed by the talentless Paul Daniels, and the follicly challenged Terry Wogan, to send us back to sleep. There is also a tribute to the remarkable Eric Morecambe, who sadly passed away earlier this year. By the time 'Escape to Victory' and Agatha Christie's 'Body in the Library' have been shown on Boxing Day, I have lost the will to live and need to go to the Britannia for a proper drink with Mark. We always used to have a family party on Boxing Day, which involved the children entertaining the grown-ups with a song or a comedy routine. My cousin Damian and I usually teamed up for the Boxing Day 'gig' and our version of Laurel and Hardy's 'Trail of the Lonesome Pine' became the stuff of legend. Unfortunately, those days are over now the kids have all grown up. Maybe we will re-introduce the Boxing Day party when the next generation comes along.

1984 has been a prolific year for celebrity deaths, as I discover while reading a newspaper article reviewing the events of the past 12 months. In January, 5 times Olympic swimming gold medallist, Johnny Weissmuller, died of a Pulmonary Edema at the age of 79. I remember him as Edgar Rice Burroughs, Tarzan the Ape Man, in about half a dozen black and white films that I watched as a young boy and seem to recall from my mother that he had a penchant for getting married. Sadly, Motown legend, Marvin Gaye, did not hear about it through the Grapevine when he was shot and killed by his father at only 44. Tommy Cooper was my favourite magician at the time of his appearance on the 'Live from Her Majesty's TV show in April, but he was gone 'just like that' when he collapsed and died on stage. Diana Dors was a blond bombshell and actress in the style of Marilyn Monroe and was only 52 when she died from Ovarian Cancer in May, just 3 years after appearing in Adam

Ant's 'Prince Charming' video. Sadly, her husband of 16 years, Alan Lake, committed suicide outside his son's bedroom 5 months later, finding it impossible to carry on life without her. Their son, Jason Dors, who once appeared in a Hammer House of Horror TV show with Diana, was only 14 years old when his mother died and must now face life without both of his parents, following his father's death. Andy Kaufman was a comedian and an Elvis impersonator who found fame in the popular American tv show 'Taxi' before he succumbed to Cancer at the age of 35. Richard Burton was a formidable Shakespearean Actor in the 1950's and early 1960's but he loved a drink and Elizabeth Taylor, failing to live up to his early promise and dying at 58 from an intracerebral haemorrhage, after years of declining health. Truman Capote, friend of Harper Lee and author of the disappointing 'In Cold Blood' died of liver cancer at only 59.

In addition, 3 popular British actors who have been TV favourites of mine, died this year. Bernard Youens who played Stan Ogden in the long running soap 'Coronation Street', died of a heart attack at 69, as did Lennard Pearce, who died this month, also at 69, after playing Grandad for many years in 'Only Fools and Horses'. The biggest surprise was the death of Leonard Rossiter who became famous for his roles as Rigsby in 'Rising Damp' and Reggie Perrin in 'The Rise and Fall'. He was only 57 when he died of a heart attack and was apparently an extremely fit man. Prime minister of India, Indira Gandhi was assassinated by two of her bodyguards at 66, while baby Fae died at only 3 weeks old after receiving a Baboons heart.

On Friday, Bev and I catch the bus to Bolton to have a look round 'the Sales' but it is just to get away from the television and we don't buy anything. The sexual tension between us increases daily but opportunities are limited in both of our parents' households. However, good news arrives when Bev's parents inform us that they will be going out on New Year's Eve. Naturally, we decide that New Year's Eve will be a good night to stay in to save some money. The plan is to have a couple of drinks and a few snacks to ensure that her parents don't return to the house unexpectedly, before moving on to more physical matters. Unfortunately, we begin foreplay by talking about our sexual history and that's when the shit hits the fan. As predicted, Bev's sexual past is a little more colourful than my own. Don't get me wrong, she has only had 3 boyfriends, one of which she didn't have sex with. However, it is the length and intensity of these relationships that are significant and give me some cause for concern. Unlike me, Bev is not in love for the first time and is now in her 4th meaningful relationship. It's not about the sex, it's about why the previous relationships broke down and the possibility of our relationship going the same way. We talk for hours as I try to make sense of why Bev sees our relationship in a different light and why ours will succeed where the others have failed. I am already aware that I am being ridiculous and ruining the evening, but I am in panic mode and scared of losing Bev. Obviously, I would have preferred it if we were both experiencing our first love together, and my heart is hurting because of this. I quiz Bev about the previous men in her life and discover that the first was a young innocent love at 16 which lasted for a year before running out of steam, the second was a first year university romance that lasted about a year and ended due to his possessiveness, while the third was a six month relationship, that was still taking place on the night that I met Bev. My head is a shed, and I am trying to digest Bev's words and understand their significance, when her parents return home, just before midnight. Immediately, they can sense the tension between us, but hang around to see in the New Year, before going to bed. I am not staying over tonight, and a taxi has already been arranged for 12.30, so I leave with Bev's firm assurance that it is me that she has loved the most. She has been very honest to me throughout the evening, but I do have a little voice inside me asking whether she enjoys falling in love and I am left to wonder whether our relationship will also end, when she gets bored.

On the way home, the taxi passes the Britannia pub and I ask the driver to stop. I try the back door of the pub and it opens, so I pay the taxi driver and enter the tap room for a late-night lock- in. Dave and Mick are in the Tap Room with Charlie while Mark and Chris are in the Lounge drinking Guinness and Snowball chasers. I order a pint of Lager and a Pernod and black. The night apparently, is still young.

The next day, the first call from a mobile phone call was 'allegedly' made in the U.K by comedian Ernie Wise, but I probably won't be purchasing one for some time. While I can see the benefits of owning a mobile phone for my love life in particular, a Motorola 8000X, with a £3000 price tag isn't a realistic option while managing on a student grant. As for Ernie Wise, he could probably afford one, but he's going to need a new job now that Eric's gone. Anyway, it looks a bit big to fit in my pocket so I can't see it catching on.

Instead, I pick up my copy of 'Vanity Fair' by William Makepeace Thackeray, to learn more about the devilishly attractive Becky Sharp and her naughty ways. I compare her briefly with Bev in my minds-eye but quickly realise what a prize pickle I have been and call Bev to apologise. We arrange to meet up for an afternoon stroll at 1.30, and I set off in a good mood after my parents tell me that they will be going to a party on Saturday and will be out all night. There is no tension between us when we meet up and I accept that my behaviour last night was unreasonable. There are no guarantees in this life and sometimes you have just got to go with the flow. We drop into the Tropics for a drink and excitedly arrange our plans for Saturday night, like a couple of lovesick kids. 'Like a Virgin' comes on the Jukebox and Bev starts singing along to It, while waving her index fingers in the air. She is taking the piss, but still manages to make me laugh. As we leave the pub 'the frog song' by Paul McCartney begins to play and I wonder if John Lennon is turning in his grave.

Before the main event of the day, on Saturday, there is the small matter of the 3rd Round of the F.A. Cup, where Manchester United are playing a Bournemouth team that knocked them out of the competition in 1984. Mark and I head for the game, both believing that a good cup run is on the agenda this year after the disappointment of last season. The game ends 3-0 in Man United's favour, but I would be lying if I said that my mind had been completely on the game. After the game Mark and I go straight home without even stopping for a celebratory drink. I need to get back home and prepare myself mentally and physically for my night of passion. I do hope that she is gentle with me.

Bev arrives at about 7.30 and shortly after my parents leave for the night, makes her excuses and disappears upstairs. She re-emerges ten minutes later dressed only in the black satin underwear that I bought her for Christmas. My heart begins beating faster as I approach her and put my hands on her bare shoulders and softly kiss her lips. I gaze down at her amazing curves, accentuated by the cut of the satin, and press my hands against her breasts. Her nipples begin to harden beneath the soft satin material, and so I bend to kiss them, moving quickly from one breast to the other to ensure that neither is neglected for more than a couple of seconds. There is room for my hand to slip inside her knickers and I gently press my finger inside her. She is already wet, and she moans as my finger enters her. I return my attention to her mouth and kiss her tenderly once more, but this time with more urgency. I can now feel the rhythm of her breathing begin to intensify, so I plunge my fingers deeper inside her and she inhales with a sharp sigh and struggles to recapture her breath. I remove her top while she struggles to remove my trousers and boxers at the same time. Both now breathing heavily, we decide to transfer proceedings to the bedroom. While following her naked bottom up the stairs I discover how difficult it is to run with an erection. We dive onto the bed, both naked and desperate for one another. I plunge myself deep inside her and she catches her breath once more before emitting a long and pleasurable moan that sounds like the well- earned relief from 3 months of sexual tension. It feels as though I am making love for the very first time and as our bodies align into one sexual frenzy, I explode inside her, and all my mind's thoughts are lost into another dimension.

The next day we go to watch the supernatural comedy film 'Ghostbusters' at the cinema and are satisfied just to be holding hands while watching the film on the large screen. Despite the fantastic reviews, the film wasn't one that particularly piqued the interest of either of us, but the special effects were good and for me it was all about spending more time with Bev. Unfortunately, the day is another day closer to Bev's return to France for her second teaching term, but I now feel more secure in our relationship and am expecting my second term to be a much smoother one.

Bev leaves for France on the following Wednesday and I begin to make plans for my return to Salford with a more positive outlook on life. Christmas was wonderful and I was already aching for Easter, but I knew there was a lot of work to be done before then, and this term I intended to remain ahead of schedule. During my final week, before starting back at university 9 striking miners were jailed for arson and the Sinclair C5 was launched.

CHAPTER 8.
AT ONE WITH THE WORLD.
January13th. - March 15th, 1985.

I was back in Salford on the evening of Sunday 13th January, focused and determined to put the failures of last term behind me. That night I didn't even go the pub.

Bev had started her term before me and would be finishing for Easter one week before I broke up, so I wanted to get ahead in my course work, so that I was prepared for her return to England. Christmas had gone extremely well, and I was completely and utterly in love. During my first week back at University I spent a record amount of time in the library and have already made notes on all on my history subjects for the second term.

Back at the flat, we have time for a couple of games of Trivial Pursuits, which is a new board game that Mark was bought for Christmas. I was leading in both games until Mark blitzed us all with his superior General Knowledge. Unfortunately, I have a weakness in the Science and Nature category, and I was lacking my little green cheese in both games. It is a good game and should be a big seller this year because everyone can play along, and the questions aren't too difficult. The four of us talk about the toys that have been big sellers over previous Christmas years and manage to come up with the Space Hopper, Action Man, Clackers, 'Etch a Sketch', Twister, Spirograph, Star War figures, Simon Says, the Sony Walkman, the Skateboard, Meccano, the Rubik's Cube, G.I Joe Figures, Care Bears, My Little Pony, and the Cabbage Patch Doll. I have received 4 of these for Christmas, but I'm not saying which ones. We are thinking, maybe Ghostbusters figures for next Christmas.

I was back in Leigh at the weekend, as Tony had invited me on his bank's Christmas Party, which was being celebrated in January due to business commitments that the bank had in December. There was to be a coach to pick us up and drop us off in Leigh and take us to the Bier Keller in Manchester. Tony and I spent most of the evening talking about our love lives and didn't really get involved with the drunken debauchery that was taking place around us. After my misdemeanour with Caroline in December I was determined to avoid trouble and not let myself down again. Of course, we did manage to drink a gallon of beer each and had a dance on the tables. There was one girl that caught my eye, and that was because she was stunning. She had blond shoulder length hair, gorgeous blue eyes and something of the Scandinavian look about her. She was wearing a lightweight navy-- blue mesh backless top and a pair of skin- tight jeans. She appeared to be with a good- looking guy who was drunk and acting like a bit of a dick. He was dancing suggestively on the table and kept flicking his beer over her head and it was clear that she was getting tired of his behaviour. I asked Tony who she was, and he told me that she was an Accounts Manager called Maria. As we boarded the coach for our journey home, I was pleased that I was in a decent state and hadn't disgraced myself again. As I took my seat towards the front of the coach Maria discreetly asked if she could sit with me. She was more softly spoken than I had expected, and her voice was almost a whisper, calm and soothing.

"Yes, that's fine, I say, boyfriend trouble?"

"Oh dear, is it that obvious, I hoped no-one had noticed".

"Don't worry, I say, it's only because I'm relatively sober".

"Yes, you seem it, why's that then?"

"Well, I've just started an important term at university and tonight was more about having a catch up with Tony".

"Ah yes, I noticed you talking to Tony, have you known him long?"

"We went to the same school in Bolton and have been good friends for about 4 years now".

"What's your name, mine is Maria".

"My name is Adam".

"Well, it's lovely to meet you Adam" she says, offering her hand.

"Do you have a girlfriend at university?"

"Yes, but she's in France at the moment".

"Why France?"

"It's part of her four- year French course, she needs to spend her 3rd year teaching in France".

"I hated languages at school, she must be a clever girl?" Don't you miss her?

"Yes, last term was difficult, but I'm hoping this term will be better".

"How long have you been together?"

"Since last September, but we've only spent a couple of months together, due to her being abroad".

"Well, at least that shows commitment, I always seem to attract the wrong sort."

"That's probably because any decent bloke would be too scared to approach you."

"What makes you say that?"

"Have you looked in the mirror lately, you're in a different league to most of us".

"Ah, what a lovely thing to say, I like you."

"I'm only being truthful, I say".

"I can tell that Adam; you've just made my night."

And so, the conversation continued.

Maria was born and bred in Derbyshire and moved to Leigh with her parents when she was 14 years old. She had worked at the bank since she was 16 and her daughter Jenny was born when she was 19, but the relationship hadn't worked out. Jenny was now 3 years old, and Maria was looking to buy her first house this year. She liked animals, especially cats, and enjoyed Motown music and Horror films. When the coach dropped me off at my parent's house Maria kissed my cheek and wished me goodnight.

'Hope to see you again", she said, as I stepped into the cold night air.

It was only a conversation, but it had been a significant one for me. It was a conversation that I would have found difficult last year, because I would have felt too self- conscious, talking to such a beautiful young woman. I was able to be myself and wasn't trying to impress Maria because I was already in a secure relationship with Bev. As it goes, I think I ended up impressing Maria because I wasn't trying. She thought I was well educated, emotionally intelligent, interesting and kind. I'm not saying she found me good looking or handsome, but I could tell that she liked me because of my personality. This was significant, because only 4 years ago I had lacked self- confidence and didn't feel as though I belonged in this insane world. I still feel at odds with my fellow human beings, but maybe being different isn't necessarily a bad thing. Yes, it was only a conversation, but I hadn't presented myself as a 'weirdo' that wanted the world to swallow him up. Don't get me wrong, I never wanted to die, but there were times when I didn't want to exist. It is not an easy life when you feel worthless and empty inside. Fortunately, four years later, I was starting to like myself.

I returned to Salford the following day and on Tuesday the four of us at Larch Court celebrated the anniversary of the Battle of Rourke's Drift. Zulu is my favourite film of all time, starring the magnificent Michael Caine and Stanley Baker who sadly passed away in 1976 aged 48. It tells the story of a small group of British soldiers tasked to build a bridge across the Buffalo River at the mission station of Rourke's Drift, which formed the border between the British colony of Natal and the Zulu Kingdom. After defeating a much larger British battalion at Isandlwana on 22nd January 1879, about 3000 Zulus diverted to Rourke's Drift to attack the station defended by just over 150 British and Colonial troops. This small force managed to repel the Zulus, despite repeated attacks that continued into the following day. Eleven Victoria Crosses were awarded to the defenders of the station, including John Chard and Gonville Bromhead, played by Baker and

Caine, respectively. There was no way of watching the film tonight, but we managed to celebrate accordingly, by starting to drink on Tuesday 22nd January when the battle began, until Wednesday, 23rd January when the battle ended. While the 3 of us raised our glasses and drank beer, Mike sipped his Coke, and pretended he was a Zulu, by throwing straws and cocktail sticks at us, instead of a four-foot assegai spear.

Zulu was released in the year I was born in 1964 and was one of many films I watched at the 'pictures' with my dad when I was a young boy. If I were to list my 20-favourite films I think that at least half of them would be from the 1960's and I wonder whether I would have been more suited to being a teenager in that era rather than the 1980's. The only film that challenges Zulu for the number 1 spot is 'The Great Escape' from 1963, but that lost its integrity by including American escapees in Stalag Luft 3, because there weren't any Americans in the camp by the time the break-out occurred. United Artists obviously thought that remarkable historical events can't take place without Americans involved and invented Steve McQueen's character to give it some relevance for the blinkered American public. What next? An American James Bond, a female Dr Who, a Black Anne Boleyn? Just how far are we prepared to go to re-invent historical facts or fiction? Other great films from the 1960's include 'The Magnificent Seven', 'Butch Cassidy and the Sundance Kid', 'The Italian Job', 'Planet of the Apes', 'Where Eagles Dare', 'The Dirty Dozen', 'Jason and the Argonauts', and 'Von Ryan's Express'. Please take a second to think about some of the great actors in each of these films. In the 1980's we must make do with the insipid Harrison

Ford, Michael Douglas, Richard Gere, Kevin Costner and Sylvester Stallone. Back in the 1960's there was Sergio Leon's trio of Spaghetti Westerns, starring Clint Eastwood, culminating with the brilliant 'The Good, the Bad, and the Ugly'; Hitchcock's disturbing thrillers like 'Psycho,' starring actors and actresses like Janet Leigh, Tippi Hedren and James Stewart; Sean Connery's 'James Bond' films and the creepy Horror stories like 'Rosemary's Baby' and Day of the Triffids'. These are all very much 'Boys Own' films that are far superior to anything that has come out in the 1980's and that includes rubbish such as Star Wars, Star Trek, Superman, Indiana Jones and Rambo. I'm not usually a fan of musicals but even 'Oliver' from 1968 was in a different League to any of that crap. You may have noticed my omission of any of the films of John Wayne from the 1960's but that's because he was a twat.

While I am considering what I have just written, I start to think about the music of the 1960's and wonder what it must have been like living through the emergence of the Beatles, the Rolling Stones, the Kinks and the Beach Boys, to name but some of the fantastic Rock and Roll Bands of the era. England had a good football team and won the World Cup in 1966 while Manchester United had Georgie Best and won the European Cup in 1968. The England cricket went 27 consecutive test matches without defeat from 1968 and the Labour Party were in power from 1964 -1970. There was also something called the 'permissive society' which I wouldn't have minded exploring on a weekend. In fact, now that I stop to consider what the 1960's had to offer its teenagers, I'm not fucking surprised I was pissed off and depressed in 1979.

On Wednesday, the 4 of us watched the first televised debate from the House of Lords, and we were all suitably unimpressed with the bunch of unelected freeloaders talking up their own self- importance, without saying anything of relevance. I can understand why the Lords may be useful but disagree with the appointing of religious members and buddies of the prime minister.

On Thursday we watched Kirsty McColl singing a Billy Bragg song called 'New England' on Top of the Pops, and while I admire Mr Bragg, I think it is only fair to add, that she sang it better than he would have done. Billy Bragg, like John Lennon, is another working- class hero of mine, because he genuinely tries to inspire change through his music and mixes his protest songs with elements of punk and folk music. Kirsty McColl is the daughter of folk singer Ewan McColl who wrote 'Dirty Old Town' a song often played by the Dubliners. I had thought that this was an old Irish song, but it is about Salford. It could just as easily have been about Leigh or a dozen other mining towns in Lancashire and Yorkshire.

On Friday evening, Mark wanted to celebrate Robbie Burns night, but we couldn't be arsed, so we just sang a couple of verses of 'Auld Lang Syne' and left it at that. We decided to go into Manchester and after a few drinks went to the cinema to watch a film called 'Terminator' starring Arnold Schwarzenegger. I was a little dubious, having previously seen another film starring Arnie, but this one suited his skill set, and I really enjoyed it. It was directed by a young Canadian guy called James Cameron who has a big future as a director if this film is anything to go by.

There was a 4th round F.A. Cup tie to get excited about on Saturday when Mark and I went to Old Trafford to see Man United defeat Coventry City by 2-1. We were cruising at one stage in the game but towards the end of the match Coventry were searching for an equaliser and we were pleased to hear the final whistle. After the match Mark and I met up with Nick and Ian for a couple of pints but took it easy as we had a Social Sciences football match on the Sunday morning and didn't want to wake up with a hangover. As it turns out we won the game 7-2 and I was delighted to score my first goal of the season, with a half volley from the edge of the box. Ian was pleased with the result and went to shake everyone's hands at the end of the game.

Ian is a lovely bloke, who always manages to make others feel good about themselves, which is a special talent. He is a great people person and I'm sure he will do well in whatever career he pursues. At the pub, he tells us about his new girlfriend called Jan, who he met at a bus stop in Liverpool. She is at York University and looks like Steffi Graf but doesn't play tennis and isn't German. It's funny that Manchester and Liverpool have such a fierce rivalry and it is well documented that the United and Liverpool fans hate each other. However, it is surprising how similar we are, and I've genuinely liked every Liverpudlian I have been introduced to. We like our music, love our football, and have a similar sense of humour, and don't mind the odd pint or eight. Many of us share a comparable working- class upbringing, and I am of the opinion, that we have far more that unites us than divides us. That they should decide to support the second greatest football team in England is neither here nor there.

On Tuesday 29th January Margaret Thatcher becomes the first post-war Prime minister to be publicly refused a degree by Oxford University and I couldn't help but smile. I really hope that Oxford win the boat race this year.

I finish 'Little Women' by the American novelist Louisa May Alcott, which is set during the American Civil War. For some reason I thought I was going to dislike the book and dismiss its author in a similar way to Jane Austen. However, I found this 'coming of age' novel featuring the four sisters, Meg, Jo, Beth, and Amy to be a classic. All four of the girls were strong believable characters who inspired and piqued my interest to such an extent that I became invested in their success. I think I will try Scott Fitzgerald and 'The Great Gatsby' next, because I do love a sexy black flapper dress.

As we eased into the month of February, I was proud of the course work I had already completed, and I was ahead of where I needed to be at this point. I was calm and relaxed about the state of my love life and felt that I was in a good place in my life. Manchester United had progressed well in the two Cup competitions and beat West Brom 2-0 on Saturday to maintain momentum in the League. The game was our closest home game to the anniversary of the Munich air disaster on the 6th of February, so Mark and I had a couple of drinks to raise a glass to the 'Busby Babes'.

On February 6th, 1958, just 3 months after Laika the dog went to space, British Airways Flight 609, carrying the Manchester United team crashed in thick snow at Munich Airport. 23 people lost their lives, including eight Manchester United footballers who were travelling home from a European Cup game in Yugoslavia. There were 21 survivors. The flight stopped to refuel in Munich and attempted to take off twice without success. On the 3rd attempt the aircraft crashed through a fence at the end of the runway and struck a house. The Manchester United players that died were Geoff Bent, Roger Bryne, Eddie Colman, Duncan Edwards Mark Jones, David Pegg, Tommy Taylor and Billy Whelan. Duncan Edwards had survived the crash but sadly died in hospital 15 days later. Johnny Berry and Jackie Blanchflower survived the crash but never played football again. The other survivors were Bobby Charlton, Bill Foulkes, Harry Gregg, Kenny Morgans, Albert Scanlon, Dennis Viollet, and Ray Wood, along with their Manager Matt Busby who had been expected to die and was given the last rites on two occasions. The crash was originally blamed on pilot error, but it was later found to have been caused by slush on the runway. There was some speculation that the club couldn't carry on but Manchester United somehow managed to rebuild itself over the next 10 years, when it successfully accomplished its destiny by winning the European Cup in 1968 with Bobby Charlton and Bill Foulkes in the team and Matt Busby as manager. I know that on this date, for the rest of my life, I will spare a thought for the Busby Babes and the rest of the passengers who tragically lost their lives in Munich. Manchester United are my football team and always will be, because the history of the club has become a part of me. The holy trinity of Best, Charlton, and Law and the European Cup win in 1968 may end up being the pinnacle of the teams footballing success, but that's irrelevant, I may sometimes despair over their attempts to replicate their successes of the past, but my ongoing support is guaranteed. Only Bryan Robson comes close to reaching the legend status of these 3 great players since Manchester United were relegated in 1974.

However, the amazing 3-0 victory Mark and I witnessed at Old Trafford against a Maradona led Barcelona, in last season's Cup Winners Cup quarter final success, did give us some hope for future optimism. It remains the best Manchester United game I have ever seen, coming two weeks after a disappointing 2.0 first leg defeat in the Bernabeu Stadium.

The letters are arriving on a regular basis from France, with Bev seemingly sharing my current euphoric state over love, life and the universe. Our relationship has felt solid since the wonderful time we spent together at Christmas and this term the time apart only seems to be making us stronger as a couple. Bev has been talking about what we might do after finishing our degrees and wonders whether I have made any concrete career plans. Bev will be studying for a teacher's qualification after finishing at university and is uncertain as to where she will complete her course, but I now feel chilled and relaxed about our future and don't have any major concerns about where we might be in 18 months' time. As for my burning career ambitions, I have nothing to aspire to as far as my family employment history is concerned. I am told that my educational qualifications point towards a career in Insurance or Banking, rather than a working-class role that I would be more familiar with. After my A- Levels, I took and passed the Civil Service entrance exam but I'm not sure whether I would be able to cope with all the political bollocks that will no doubt come with the territory.

On Valentine's Day, instead of going out for a romantic meal and showering my beloved with roses, I sit watching Top of the Pops again, with Mark, Nick, and Mike. Morrissey and the Smiths are performing 'How soon is now' and I start thinking that it's probably not soon enough. I go to the telephone box to call Bev, but she is out.

The following day Manchester United beat Blackburn Rovers 2-0 in the F.A. Cup 5th Round tie at Ewood Park and the F.A Cup dream for 1985 remains alive.

On Tuesday the 19th of February a new soap begins on BBC1 called Eastenders and we all watch the opening episode in the flat. Mark sums it up as 'a load of cockney shit' and while I agree with him, it will probably go down well in the south.

Walking back to the flat on Thursday evening I catch up with Mark and it becomes apparent that he needs a beer or two. He suggests going to the Strawberry Duck which is a 30-minute train journey from Salford situated in Entwistle, originally a township in the chapelry of Turton which in turn was part of the ecclesiastical parish of Bolton. As we walk into the small train station, we are surprised to find our train ready to depart and so we decide that this must be fate and step aboard. Entwistle railway station is situated between Darwen and Bromley Cross railway stations on the line between Blackburn and Bolton and is a 'request stop'. Nearby are the Wayoh and Turton and Entwistle Reservoirs and the area is popular with walkers, anglers and doggers. Other than these local attractions the Strawberry Duck is probably the main reason why people get off at Entwistle, because there is fuck all else to do there. As we step inside the pub we are greeted with the sound of music and the clicking of balls from the pool table, where a couple of young girls are attempting to master the overly long snooker cues and giggling at their own shortcomings. They look up and smile at us as we walk towards the bar and order a couple of pints of Thwaites IPA. We briefly consider challenging the girls to a game of pool but are drawn to the music coming from the Lounge area. In the Lounge we are surprised to find the 3 musicians playing their instruments while sitting down at a couple of tables with their beers close at hand, rather than the informal option of the stage in the corner of the room. They look over at us as we take our seats and the one without a beard asks us if we want a couple of Kazoos to blow into. It would have been churlish to refuse so we accept the challenge and begin to create a cacophony of wonderful sound together. All the blowing makes us extra thirsty, so we quickly need a top up and Mark suggests a pint of Theakston's Old Peculiar to put some hair on our chests.

The evening takes a surprising turn when a classmate from our Bolton school days turns up at the pub with his girlfriend. As it turns out, the girlfriend is his wife and they already have two children, the first of which was fathered by another man. It is bizarre to think that we were in the same class as Andrew less than 4 years ago and that he is now living the life of a family man with a small, terraced house in Darwen, purchased by his parents when Carole became pregnant for the second time. Andrew isn't working just now, but Carole has a part time job in a café in Darwen, owned by her parents, who also act as willing babysitters when they both need some free time. Andrew is busy thinking about writing a novel but is still in the 'ideas stage' at the current time. He is still as funny and quick witted as I remember him at school and the banter between the two of them is amusing but I can't help but think that this is not the life that he or his parents would have wished for when he passed his 11 plus exam and went to grammar school in 1976. I could be wrong, and this could be the path Andrew has carefully chosen to provide an ever- lasting meaning to his earthly existence, but I doubt it.

We chat merrily away and happily blow our kazoos as instructed until it is time for Mark and me to catch the last train back to Salford while Andrew and Carole return to relieve the babysitters from looking after their children back in Darwen.

The following Wednesday, England beat Northern Ireland 1-0 in another World Cup qualifier with a goal from Mark Hateley, who somehow finds himself playing for A.C Milan and on Friday, Patrick Magee is charged with murder as a result of the bomb he planted at the Brighton Hotel, which exploded during the Conservative Party Conference.

As these events are taking place, another week quickly passes by. I am maintaining a good pace with my term's work and my re-union with Bev is inching closer. Madonna is on Top of the Pops singing 'Material Girl' and I think back to Christmas and Bev mimicking the 'Like a Virgin' song at the Tropics. I smile to myself and think about getting my hands on her sexy little body again, in a little over two weeks.

This week I have been focused on some tutorial work, that I need to complete for my excellent Contemporary History course. We have been covering the 2nd World War and the tutorial examined Adolph Hitler's commitment to expanding Germanys living space. Key to this was the 'Jewish question' and Hitler's prophecy in 1939 that predicted their annihilation in the event of a new World War. The history of the 3rd Reich teaches us about the evil human beings are capable of when the rule of law breaks down, and Nazi Germany systematically murdered six million Jews, through a policy of extermination in concentration camps. The Nazis agreed the Final Solution to the Jewish question in January 1942 and the killing continued until the end of the 2nd World War in Europe, in May 1945.

In my research, I came across the crazy Holocaust deniers and their assertion that the Holocaust did not happen or was greatly exaggerated. Anyone who believes that extermination camps and gas chambers weren't used for the genocidal mass murder of Jews is ignoring the overwhelming historical evidence to the contrary.

I did however, come across numerous articles written around the time of the 1st world war that referred to the suffering of 6 million Jews. With my interest piqued, I came across more information relating to an ancient religious prophecy in the Torah which stated that 'before the Jewish people could reclaim and reconquer Palestine and establish a Jewish homeland called 'Israel', 6 million Jews would have to perish. As a self- confessed cynic, with no belief in God or Religion, the 6 million number began to concern me. It seemed like there were too many people invested in making the 6 million number tie in with the ancient religious prophecy, and this bothered me. If the number was lower or higher than the 6 million quoted, I would sooner know the truth. As I have already stated, ancient religious prophecies mean fuck all to me, especially when I see that the 6 million number has been bandied around for decades, prior to the 2nd World War. Consequently, I need to ask the question in good faith as to whether the figure of 6 million Jewish deaths during the 2nd World War, confirms the accuracy of an ancient religious prophecy, or whether it is a convenient estimation? I decide not to mention my findings during the tutorial because debate on such matters, however genuine, doesn't usually go well.

The miner's strike comes to an end on the 3rd of March, after a struggle lasting a year and involving 142, 000 miners. It feels as though we are moving towards the end of an era, not just for coal mining but for our proud working-class population. I am sad for the communities of Yorkshire decimated by the events of the past year, knowing it won't be long before the remaining pits in Leigh are also closed.

On Wednesday, Mark and I go to watch Manchester United beat Videoton 1-0 in a close Quarter Final encounter in the Cup Winners Cup at Old Trafford. The return leg is in a couple of weeks and promises to be a tight affair, unlike the openness of the 2 games played against Dundee United, in the last round. On a positive note, we beat Dundee United after a home draw, so there is no reason why we can't beat the Hungarians.

Three days later and it's another Quarter Final game, this time in the F.A. Cup and a 4-2 win over West Ham United takes us into the semi- finals. There seemed to be a bit of trouble taking place in the West Ham end of the ground, but we didn't find out what the problem was. As for the semi- final, Mark and I have seen enough F.A. Cup draws to know that we will be facing Liverpool.

Two IRA members are jailed for the 1981 bombing campaign which included the attack on Chelsea Barracks, which killed 2 passing civilians and injured another 40 people, including 23 British soldiers. A bomb disposal expert called Kenneth Robert Howarth was also killed, trying to defuse an IRA bomb on Oxford Street, in London. Sadly, more pointless waste of life that could have been avoided with a little common sense from the politicians.

An Egyptian man named Mohammed Al Fayed has bought Harrods, but it's unlikely that I will meet him, because it's not one of the shops I buy my gear from, at the present time. While the newspapers present a rather mixed opinion about Mohammed, I have no reason to believe that he is anything other than an upstanding citizen, whose business interests in Haiti, Dubai and Brunei were all legitimate and above board, as was his relationship with Saudi Arabian arms dealer Adrian Khashoggi. Some newspapers are so quick to make snap judgements about a person. Sadly, I don't have any friends or relatives that currently shop at

Harrods, but Michael Jackson seems to be doing well for himself these days, while Princess Diana seems to be partial to a nice frock or two, so I think Mohammed will do ok.

In Salford, John has been to a new club in Manchester called the Hacienda. He has been to see 'the Pogues' and the 'Associates' and reckons that both bands were good, while the club was excellent. Apparently, the lead singer of the Pogues is a' bit of a looker'. John tells me that the Hacienda has something to do with the band 'New Order' who did the excellent 'Blue Monday' a couple of years ago. The group was formed after the death of Ian Curtis who was the vocalist for 'Joy Division', a Salford band formed in 1976. Both Peter Hook and Bernard Sumner from the band, were born in Broughton, where we went for a night out in October, and I lived during my first year at university. The founder of the club is another Salford lad called Tony Wilson, who I have seen on Granada Reports, alongside Richard Madeley and Judy Finnegan. Tony founded Factory Records in 1978 along with Alan Erasmus, Rob Gretton and Martin Hannett and seems to have a genuine interest in promoting the Manchester area, as opposed to simply benefiting from it.

John loves his live music and like Mark will go to watch a promising new band, anytime, anyplace, anywhere. He has started to see the red headed girl from Larch Court that he met at Christmas, but no-one has a nice word to say about her. Mark says that she has got a face like a bulldog chewing a wasp, but Nick thinks Mark is being too kind.

On Monday 11th March 1985 Mikhail Gorbachev becomes leader of the Soviet Union following the death of Konstantin Chernenko. With his appointment there seems to be an opportunity to reach out and hope for an end to the arms race, and a more democratic Soviet Union in the future. The Soviet Union appears weaker now that at any other time since World War 2 and while this adds to the hope of an improved relationship with the Russians, there will never be trust.

Mark's 20th birthday is on Wednesday, and we go out for a few drinks to the Flemish Weaver with Nick and Ian. Ian tells us that he and Jan are going to 'Aintree' on Friday 29th March to watch the horse-racing, and can pick us up some extra tickets, if we are interested. The tickets are for Ladies Day, which is the day before the Grand National event, so it would be brilliant to take Bev. Nick is keen, and Mark and I ask Ian to get us 5 tickets, thinking that Chris and Colin would also like to go.

Most of my terms work is done, by the 15th of March, so I head back home to Leigh for a night out with the lads and we celebrate Mark's birthday again. Chris and Paul are the only ones out tonight as Colin is in Wales for another week and Tony is working on Saturday morning. Mark and I still have one more week until the end of term, but Bev finishes today and will be home tomorrow. Tonight, however, is about Mark and we go to the Britannia to watch Manchester United play West Ham United at Upton Park, in a League game. We arrive at 7 o'clock but some of the regulars must have been here for a couple of hours, based on the silly looking grins on their faces. The game is exciting and ends in a 2-2 draw which Mark and I accept as a decent result. We then go into Leigh and call in on another four or five pubs before I decide to call it a night. Paul asks us to put the date of 4th May in our diaries, as he is arranging a Eurovision Party at his house. The 3 of us aren't sure what we are supposed to do at a Eurovision Party but there was going to be food and beer, so we weren't complaining.

CHAPTER 9.
THERE MAY BE
TROUBLE AHEAD.
March 16th-April 14th 1985.

Bev finishes her second term in France one week before Mark and I finish in Salford and is safely back in Leigh by Saturday afternoon. On Saturday evening we go out with Tony and Susan but don't stay out late as Bev is tired from her journey home. We also want to spend some time alone discussing our plans for next week. We decide that Bev will join me in Salford for a few days,' and so, the following evening, we set off excited at the prospect of spending some quality time together, without being in our parents' pockets. It is St Patrick's day, so Mark drags us all off to the Church for a Guinness or two. There are a few Irish folk already celebrating, and it isn't long before the singing starts, and a fiddle appears, accompanied by the stamping of feet. The fiddle is then joined by a flute and whistle, and we all marvel over the men's fingering techniques. Mike is enjoying the music and starts clapping his hands before standing up to do a little Irish jig, for which he receives generous applause from the pub clientele. Mike has been kind enough to sort out

Bev and I with some tickets for a club he is going to next Tuesday in Manchester, and it turns out to be a Northern Soul event. Northern Soul isn't something that either of us have previously enjoyed but we are open to new experiences and looking forward to making a night of it.

On Monday, we go to watch Beverley Hills Cop at the cinema. It was a great film and Eddie Murphy is proving to be a top 'box -office star', and we find him hilarious. I saw 'Trading Places' last year and thought that it was one of the best films I have ever seen, so it's not all bad in the 1980's, after all. My dad says Eddie Murphy is just like Richard Pryor who won many awards for comedy in the 70's and early 80's, but I think Eddie Murphy is probably the future. Also, of note was the 'Axel F' synth pop theme that ran throughout the film composed by German musician and composer Harold Faltermeyer. For some reason I'd got it into my brain that it was Greek musician 'Vangelis' that had composed the music, but I checked and realised that he was best known for composing scores to Chariots of Fire in 1981, as well as Blade Runner in 1982, Antarctica in 1983 and The Bounty in 1984.

Tuesday evening arrives and it turns out that we like Northern Soul more than we thought and we are gobsmacked by the energy levels on the dance floor. Mike is jumping and twisting and turning on the dance floor, and his dance moves are incredible. This probably explains why he is so slim and athletically built. It turns out that Mike was a 'bit of a lad' before he became a born- again Christian. He used to go over to Wigan Casino in the late 1970's, when he could only have been 14 or 15, to attend Northern Soul all-nighters. He said that his friends would take amphetamines to keep them dancing throughout the night but that no-one drank alcohol because it would have caused dehydration. Instead, they took bottles of water to maintain their fluid levels. One night, a much older girl took him outside for sex, but he didn't know what he was supposed to be doing. Mike described the encounter as trying to stick a marshmallow into a penny slot. Bev couldn't stop laughing and said that it was one of the best nights out that she has ever had. On the way home I had to carry her part of the way because her feet were hurting from all the dancing. It turns out that high heels aren't the best footwear to use when dancing to Northern Soul, but we will know for next time. During the evening I recognised the songs 'Tainted Love' and 'Sugar Pie Honey Bunch', by the 4 Tops, but was informed that these songs were a bit too mainstream now. On the way home Mike was talking about the 'Twisted Wheel' in Manchester, which was a famous Northern Soul venue before it was closed- down. Wigan Casino has also been closed since 1981, so I am guessing that fans of Northern Soul now depend on one off gigs like tonight to keep on dancing. Bev and I weren't on the dance floor for nearly as much time as Mike, but our legs were hurting in the morning.

After a wonderful 3 days and nights together in Salford, Bev goes home on Wednesday lunchtime, so that I could wrap up a few loose ends, before the end of term. Living together, albeit briefly, had been a liberating experience, compared with being in Leigh at our parent's homes. We got on terrifically well and an easy- going relationship was now developing between us with no dominant partner.

Sadly, Manchester United lost 1-0 to Videoton on Wednesday night and with the game tied after two legs went out of the Cup Winners Cup 5-4 on penalties. However, on a brighter note Nick has picked up the Aintree tickets from Ian, so we are excited about going to our first Day at the Races.

Unfortunately, for Mark and me, the excitement is short lived. On Friday evening, we receive the terrible news that Colin's father has died of a heart attack on Thursday night. It is devastating for the family, and I call Colin to see how he is coping. He was still in Wales when he received the news and said that the journey home was awful, and that he just wanted to burst into tears. His brother is also home from university in Loughborough, so they are doing their best to console their mother, while dealing with their own grief.

Manchester United got back to winning ways by beating Aston Villa 4-0 on Saturday afternoon, but I was feeling a little down all day because of the awful news about Colin's father and I just couldn't settle. I tried reading through the newspapers to occupy my mind and realised from all the red and white flags on display, that it was St George's Day. I don't know much about St George other than he slayed a dragon and saved a princess, so I thought I would do a bit of research to distract myself. I found out that he was born in Turkey in 280 A.D and died in 303 A.D, so he didn't have a long and saintly life and probably didn't slay a dragon, because they don't exist. He must have done something good because he was also the Patron Saint of Greece and Portugal and Russia, so he was well travelled. He was a soldier in the Roman Army which probably explains how he managed to get about a bit, and he was a Christian which may have made him unpopular with his fellow Romans. As for the Dragon, it was described as half animal and half fish, so it was probably a crocodile that he killed, which the locals had been feeding two sheep a day to prevent it from getting peckish. This might have taken place in the Middle East or North Africa or possibly Berkshire, which makes me wonder whether it is time to appoint another Patron Saint of England

On Sunday, I was eager to spend my first Easter with Bev. My mum and dad would be working for most of the following week, so Bev and I would be able to spend some time alone at my parents' house. This would allow us to relax in each other's company which hadn't really been possible over Christmas. Along with the time spent together in Salford, it soon started to feel that Bev and I were settling into a normal relationship and on Monday we took advantage of some 'alone time' to trespass repeatedly on one anothers 'personal space'.

We find out on Monday night that the Funeral for Colin's Dad is going to be on Friday, so Bev and I go to meet Mark and Chris on Tuesday morning to decide what to do about going to Aintree. Colin doesn't know that we have bought him a ticket for the event, and it will be the last thing on his mind now, but we need to decide if the four of us can enjoy a day at the races, when our friend will be struggling to get through his dad's funeral. We buy a Sympathy card for all the lads to sign, and I agree to call Colin, to find out more details about the funeral. During the conversation, I mention the tickets for the races trip, and Colin is adamant that we all go and enjoy the day. He says that he wasn't expecting the lads to go to the funeral and is touched that everyone has been thinking of him and his family.

On Friday, Bev, Mark, Chris and I meet at Leigh Bus and Coach station. The lads are all suited and booted, wearing collar and tie, and ready for the day ahead. We make the ten-minute walk to St Joseph's Church and take our seats at the back of the church. The service is lovely but incredibly sad, all of us no doubt thinking about how awful it would be, if one of our own parents had died so young. The first reading is done by Colin's father's younger brother who appears visibly shaken by his brother's death and struggles to make it through to the end of his piece of scripture. To our surprise, it is Colin who does the Eulogy and his words about his father are poignant and loving, honouring a gentle man who has worked hard throughout his life, to provide for his family. There are tears wept by relatives and friends, but Colin's voice doesn't waver, and he does his family and his friends proud. After the service is over, Colin thanks us for coming and invites us for drinks and sandwiches back at the house. He is clearly moved by our presence at the church, and we are pleased to have made the correct decision, by attending the funeral. We go back to his house for a light bite to eat but don't stay long, leaving the family to their privacy while they mourn their sad loss.

On Saturday lunchtime Bev and I are still feeling the effects of yesterday's emotions and decide to go into Leigh for a bite to eat and a few drinks. We end up watching the Grand National in the Britannia and put some money on Corbierre, who had won the race in 1983 and was being ridden by Peter Scudamore. West Tip and Greasepoint were the favourites for the race, but West Tip fell at Becher's Brook while Greasepoint came fourth. Last Suspect, a 50-1 outsider, ridden by Hywel Davies won the race in a time of 9 minutes and 42.7 seconds, while Corbierre finished the race in a respectable 3rd place. I am delighted to report that no horses died as a result of the 1985 Grand National but I am worried about the size of 'Becher's Brook' which still looks dangerous and must be jumped twice during the race. Whilst we would have enjoyed our Day at the Races tremendously, neither of us are big fans of horse-racing, which cannot be said for most of the pub's hysterical customers here today. Despite this, the Grand National has always had a special memory for me since I picked out 'Red Rum' in a sweepstake at my dad's football club in 1973 and won him some money. I can still picture the excitement on the day, as our horse came from 30 lengths behind to win the race. Red Rum became a legend and quite possibly the greatest horse to ever win the Grand National. He retained his title in 1974 carrying 12 stone in weight and followed this with victory at the Scottish Grand National, later the same year. Red Rum was placed 2nd in 1975 to 'L'Escargot' (who sadly died last year) and in 1976 to 'Rag Trade' (who died at the 1978 Grand National), before winning his 3rd Grand National in 1977, in what must be regarded as one of the greatest moments in horse racing history. Red Rum appeared on the Sports Personality of the Year awards later that year and clearly recognised the voice of his jockey Tommy Stack who was appearing by video link from another location. Red Rum retired the following year with his victory time of 9 minutes and 19 seconds in 1973, still the fastest ever run. A truly remarkable horse who loved Aintree. The following day, again in Liverpool, Man United won 1-0 at Anfield, to put a big dent in Liverpool's hopes of winning the League this year.

On Monday, Bev began some part time work at a different Care Home in Leigh while I started to read 'A Picture of Dorian Grey' by Oscar Wilde, which is a short book and shouldn't take long to read. I had finished 'The Great Gatsby' but felt it was over hyped American trash. Maybe I am being harsh, but 'one of the best books ever written?', do me a favour!

On Good Friday, Bev and I went to a family gathering at my cousin Catherine's new home in Bolton, with my mum and dad. There are 16 of us crammed into the tiny house with Catherine and Mick's parents, and 4 of my cousins, all with their partners, fighting for somewhere to sit. We had a few drinks and some good food, and I was able to show off Bev to my relatives, for the first time. On the way home Bev suggested that I grow a moustache, so I think I will give it a go. The following day we go out for some lunch in Leigh and visit the George and Dragon and the Boars Head. I show Bev the stubble already forming above my top lip, but she doesn't seem overly impressed.

In the interests of fairness, Easter Sunday is spent at Bev's parents, and I get to see Bev's sister's baby girl for the first time. Bev's sister is 3 years older and starting to look like her mother, so I'm hoping this trait doesn't run in the family. The baby girl is called Sophie and she is ever so cute. I am given the responsibility of holding her while her mother goes into the kitchen, and she looks me in the eyes and giggles. The bonding is instantaneous, and I feel immediately protective of this little girl sitting in my arms, but I'm in no rush to have one of my own, anytime soon.

The main event taking place over Easter, other than the Resurrection of Christ, is Beverly's 21st Birthday, and I have been trying to convince her to have a party. However, Bev has decided on a quiet meal at a posh restaurant in Farnworth, with only me and her parents in attendance. It's not what I would have gone for, but Bev is not from a big family, and I've only ever met 3 of her girlfriends. While she appears confident and is very articulate, I don't think she likes being the centre of attention and isn't the party girl that I first thought. Clearly, I'm still learning about the real Bev. I have also noticed that while she is extremely comfortable talking to the boys, she isn't as relaxed in the company of other girls. I am however, pleased that my own self- confidence is developing when I talk to new people, and it is Bev that I can thank for that.

As it turns out, we all have a lovely meal and Bev opens the presents that we have taken along to the restaurant. I have bought her perfume and a Phil Collins record, while her parents have got her an expensive watch to mark the occasion. It is a relaxed affair, that will bear no resemblance to my 21st in September, when I will be gathering all my friends and family and getting absolutely bladdered. I am delighted that my moustache is taking shape and that Bev likes it, but less pleased that Manchester United have lost 1.0 to Sheffield Wednesday today. Tonight, I am staying over at Bev's and wonder if she will sneak into my room for a touch of 'Midnight Delight' or a 'Big Birthday Bang', but she doesn't.

On Thursday, an 18 months old boy, becomes the youngest person in the U.K to die of AIDs, which I'm assuming was either passed on from the mother or was due to a blood transfusion, but I'm not sure. There are a lot of mixed messages circulating about the causes of this disease and more action is required to clarify the situation. I am aware that many young men have died in the United States and while this currently seems to be less of an issue in the U.K, we need more information. While news is consistently bubbling beneath the surface, there seems to be a reluctance for the politicians to address the problem face on, but no surprise there. There will be concerns for haemophiliacs that blood supplies could be contaminated with the virus, while drugs users sharing needles is another bone of contention. As a straight man, I also have concerns and I think that anyone who dismisses the illness as a 'gay' disease is deluding themselves. From what I have learned, there are women carrying the virus who are neither drug users, haemophiliacs or promiscuous and it only takes one unfortunate decision to ruin a life. I can only practise safe sex in the hope that I haven't already made that lethal error of judgement.

Two weeks after the funeral, the 4 guys that had meant to be going to the races, have arranged a lad's road trip to Blackpool. Chris has bought himself a car and is taking Mark, Colin and I to the Vegas of the Northwest. We are heading for the Pleasure beach for a Roller Coaster bonanza, and I don't care how old we are. On the way up the M6 to Blackpool Chris has the car radio turned up to party mode and we sing along to the tunes with a can of Stones beer in our hands. 'You spin me round' by Dead or Alive comes on the radio and its only when you put beer and your best mates together, that you realise what a brilliant song it is. Even 'Heavy Rock' Mark is inspired by the tune, and the journey flies by. The guys are taking the piss over my new moustache, but they're only jealous at how good I look with my new facial addition.

On arrival, we all buy a Pleasure beach Party ticket, which allows us to go on different graded rides for a fraction of the cost. First stop however, is the Donkey Derby game, where you are required to roll balls into holes scoring 1 point, 2 points or 3 points for which your horse will move forward one space for every point. The first horse to cross over to the other side is the winner for which you are awarded tickets to enable you to buy prizes from the attached shop. I used to play the game a lot as a child and my first 3 games all result in wins, for which I am presented with a handful of tickets. I start to get a disapproving look from the guy running the stall and decide to move on in order to give the children a fair chance. I buy a cute Teddy bear for Bev from the shop with my tickets and we move on to the Big Dipper. Before we leave the Pleasure beach, we go on the Waltzer and we are sent dizzy to the tune 'You spin me round' which for reasons unknown, seems to be a big favourite for this ride. We have a few beers and then go for chips on the beachfront and take a stroll down the promenade, playing on a few of the slot machines, which are the same slot machines I played on in the early 1970's. The tide is coming in and there isn't a donkey in sight, but there is time to go for an ice-cream before we go home. We had planned on staying a little longer, but Chris wants to get back to Leigh so that he can get rid of the car and have a few beers. Personally, I'm quite pleased because I can call Bev and arrange to meet up later. We have had a great day with plenty of laughs, so Chris deserves a few beers after driving us to Blackpool and back.

As soon as I arrive home, I call Bev, but she has already arranged to go out with Scarlett. I say we can meet up for a few drinks in Leigh later, but she tells me they are going to stay local rather than make the trip into town. While this sounds perfectly reasonable, I am suspicious of Bev's tone which comes across as nervy and a little tense.

"Which pub are you going to", I ask.

"I don't know", Bev snaps back.

"I'm only asking", I say.

"Well, I didn't know you'd be back so early".

"Neither did I, that's why I thought I'd give you a call".

"I'm ok with you seeing Scarlett and I'm happy to go out with the lads, it's not a problem".

"Ok, she says, I'm going to need to get ready now".

"Have a nice night", I manage to say, just before she puts the phone down.

As I shower, I think about Bev's strange behaviour and by the time I set off for the Britannia, I am convinced that she is lying.

The following morning, I wake up determined to get to the bottom of last night's moody phone call with Bev, so I call her and arrange to meet her for a drink at

1.00p.m. On meeting her at the George and Dragon, I am direct and to the point.

"Why were you lying to me last night", I say. She isn't expecting this approach and her face tells me everything that I need to know. I go straight for the jugular.

"You weren't out with Scarlett last night, were you?"

"No", she admits timidly.

"Ok, we're getting somewhere, who were you with then?"

"Stephen" she says, "he phoned up at teatime yesterday and asked if we could meet up".

"Stephen, your first boyfriend?"

"Yes", Bev replies.

"Why is he phoning you?"

"He sent me a 21st birthday card, so I dropped him a note to thank him".

"And?"

"Well, he phoned up and asked me out".

"And you decided to go without telling me about it?"

"I didn't think it through, I just wanted to see if he'd changed."

"And had he?" I ask angrily.

"Not really, nothing happened".

"Oh, did you want something to happen?"

"No, I don't even fancy him anymore."

I was quiet for a moment, trying to digest what she had told me. The thought of my own indiscretion at Christmas flashed through my mind and I was unsure about what to say next. I decided on:

"And will you be seeing him again?"

"No, I told him I was with you now."

If Bev was telling me the truth, I could understand why she may have been curious to see Stephen, but she had lied to me once already and had all night to come up with a believable story. I was hurt and I was angry, but I had a decision to make. Do I accept what Bev has told me, or do I continue with the argument and potentially make matters worse? My main concern is regards timing, as Bev is due to leave for France tomorrow and won't be back for 6 weeks. I do want to question her more, but she is crying and apologising for what she has done and promises me that it will never happen again. There is something inside me telling me that something like this will happen again, but I can't stand the thought of remaining mad at her for 6 weeks, while we are apart, and so I decide to accept her apology and move on. I wonder whether this was how her previous relationships broke down and consider whether Bev could be getting bored with our relationship. However, I make the decision to kiss and make up, and so we do. I have an extremely important term ahead of me and will be taking 5 exams next month that will contribute 40% to my final degree. I need to focus all my energy over the next 7 weeks to give myself the best chance of success with these exams, and it will be a testing time. I have listened to Bev's reasons for meeting up with Stephen and have accepted her apologies and her assurances that she loves me. Bev tells me that she will write to me every week and make up for her actions during the summer holidays, when we can devote more of our time to each other and get away on a sunny holiday, with just the two of us. This does sound amazing and is something that I can hold on to during the difficult weeks of studying that lie ahead. However, while I am optimistic about her promises, I am beginning to realise that being 'cautiously optimistic' is more prudent where Bev is concerned.

Due to the drama of the day, I miss out on the important football match taking place this afternoon. I discover that Manchester United have drawn 2-2 with Liverpool in the F.A. Cup Semi-Final and a replay will be required to see which of the two teams make it to Wembley in May.

CHAPTER 10.
TESTING TIMES.
April 15th- June 3rd 1985.

I return to Salford on the Monday morning and go straight to my first lecture of the week. This term will be a short one for me, made up of a limited number of lectures, a few tutorials and no essays, as we will be focusing on revision and the passing of 5 crucial exams. I get a few Hail Hitler remarks because of my moustache but am now largely oblivious to the comments and just say "Yeah yeah," and move on. On Wednesday Mark and I are overjoyed when Manchester United beat Liverpool 2-1 in the F.A Cup semi-final replay and cement their place at Wembley on the 18th of May, where they will face Everton in the 104th F.A Cup Final. We have been anticipating this since the 3rd Round draw was made, and we are delighted that Man United now have the chance to win the cup again, just 2 years after beating Brighton 4-0 in the 1983 F.A Cup Final replay.

However, by Friday my mood has changed as I start to mull over Bev's deceitful behaviour during Easter, and negative thoughts begin to fill my head regarding the state of our relationship. How good can our relationship be if Bev feels the need to see Stephen again, whilst deceiving me about it. Can she really love me as much as she claims, or could the spark be gradually flickering out of our relationship? It is now April 15th, and my first exam is only 5 weeks away, on May 23rd. I collect all my books together, along with the notes and essays that I will need to study for my exams, but the required levels of application for study are missing. My brain is working over-time, I can't concentrate and I'm not sleeping. I manage to spend some time on a revision plan for each of my exams, but this is nothing more than a delaying tactic and I fall further behind. Another week passes by, and I still haven't heard from Bev or started my revision.

It is Sunday before I make a concerted effort to revise for my Micro- Economics exam, but progress is slow as my mind starts to wander. I read the material in front of me and then read it again becoming frustrated that the words aren't building a better relationship with my brain. I decide to watch a bit of TV, and stumble across the World Snooker Championship final between Steve Davis and Dennis Taylor. I've never been a big snooker fan and it's not a sport that I've ever got into playing, as I prefer to be outdoors. I have always admired Alex Higgins who won the tournament in 1972 and then more memorably for me in 1982, but that's about as far as my interest in the game has gone. Nick and Ian have an ongoing competition that stands at about 18 frames each, but I've never been tempted to join them. Steve Davis has already won the Championship in 1981, 1983 and 1984 and is the clear favourite for retaining his title this year. The best of 35 frames is split into four sessions and Steve Davis takes a commanding 7-0 lead in the first session and appears to be easing his way to his 4th title. However, Dennis Taylor fights his way back into the game and ends the second session at 9-7 down and the 3rd session at 13-11 down. It was during the fourth session on Sunday evening that the match really started to get interesting, when Taylor managed to tie the match at 17-17 with just the deciding frame to be played. As the evening session progressed, it was clear that all four of us in the flat had become engrossed by the game and were all on tenterhooks, supporting Dennis Taylor as the underdog. There were shouts of encouragement and whoops of delight, coming from all four corners of the flat, followed by angry swear words when Steve Davis appeared to be getting on top. The tension became unbearable as the final frame came to its dramatic conclusion. The 35th frame of the game lasted 68 minutes and Davis was leading 62-44 with only the last 4 coloured balls on the table. However, as the clock eased past midnight Taylor potted the brown, the blue and the pink to trail by only 3 points with only the black to pot. Each player then took 3 shots each at the black and missed the pot but Davis on his 3rd attempt left the ball in a very potable position. As Taylor made his way to the table all four of us in the flat held our breaths as he sunk the black ball to win the match. It was 12.23a.m. When Dennis Taylor raised his cue above his head and waved his finger at someone in the audience, the whole flat erupted with wild excitement and celebration at what was surely the most enthralling snooker final in the history of the game. All four of us were dancing about and running up and down the stairs, and into one another's rooms. At one point a mini conga was undertaken outside the flat, along the corridor of the 3rd floor at Larch Court. The neighbours, no doubt, would have been angry, if they had any work to go to in the morning.

I slept well that night and woke up feeling refreshed and ready to take on my revision with renewed vigour. All because of a stupid game of snooker.

That week England drew 0-0 with Romania, Wigan beat Hull 28-24 in an exciting Rugby League Silk Cup Challenge Final, Manchester United beat Norwich City 1-0 at Carrow Road and Leigh were relegated from the 1st Division of the Rugby League Championship, only 3 years after winning the title. I am pleased to report that I watched none of it. Mark and I didn't even go to Paul's Eurovision Party, but we apologised, and he gracefully accepted our reasons. Bobby socks from Norway won the competition in Sweden despite Norway usually finishing last with 'null' points. The UK's entry came a respectable fourth. Chris went to the party and reported back to us that Paul and Teabag had dressed up in a couple of lavish costumes and that the party had been a great night with lots of girls from their gym joining in the fun. I smiled to myself and continued with my revision.

Manchester United had another couple of wins against Nottingham Forest and Queens Park Rangers, but this was overshadowed by a fire at the Bradford City stadium that killed 56 spectators and injured at least 265. The stadium was well known for its antiquated design which included a main stand with a wooden roof, and warnings had been given about a build- up of litter below the seats in the stand. The match was the final game of the season for Bradford City against Lincoln City and was supposed to be a celebration of their successful season, with Bradford receiving the 3rd Division trophy before the match. It took less than 4 minutes for the entire stand to be engulfed in flames and by then the disaster was unavoidable. No-one should ever go to watch a sporting event and lose their lives. My heart goes out to the city and the people of Bradford. Sadly, on the same day, a 14-year-old boy died in Brighton, as a result of Leeds football hooligans.

The revision continues and I begin to feel more positive about the upcoming exams. Manchester United lose their last game of the season 5-1 at Watford, but I don't really care, because they now have 'bigger fish to fry' in the FA Cup Final. Everton have already won the League and they complete a Double by beating Rapid Wien in the European Cup Winners Cup Final on my dad's 43rd Birthday. If they beat Manchester United on Saturday, they will win an historic treble, but I am convinced that this won't happen.

On Thursday, two days before the Cup Final, 2 South Wales miners, get life imprisonment for the murder of a taxi driver and I finally get my first letter of the term from Bev. She has decided to delay her return to the U.K by 11 days, so that she can spend some time with her new friends exploring Paris and celebrating the end of term. She has decided that this is a good idea that will enable me to concentrate on my exams and maintain my focus during what will be a testing time. While this may sound reasonable, being that I have five exams over twelve days, it doesn't seem like it to me, considering the promises she made when she left for France last month. Sometimes, a man just needs his woman to prove that she is committed to him, even if this means coming home and just talking on the phone for the next couple of weeks.

However, on Saturday, the F.A Cup Final is all that matters, and Bev doesn't exist for the next 24 hours. All the lads are in the Britannia early doors and the atmosphere is electric. Overall, support is slightly favouring Manchester United but there are enough Everton supporters and Man Utd haters in the pub to create a bit of tension. There is plenty of banter amongst the 2 sets of supporters and a great deal of alcohol being consumed, but it won't kick off. The worst that is going to happen today, is total humiliation at the hands of the opposition, and there is a real possibility that Manchester United could be outclassed by Everton. Everton have won the title at a canter this season and added a European trophy to their cabinet this week. They are also the current holders of the F.A Cup having beaten Watford in the final last year. Manchester United only managed a 4th place finish this year and were hammered 5-1 by Watford in their last game, so the omens are bad. They failed to beat Everton in 3 attempts this season, losing 5-0 and 2-1 while managing a 1-1 draw at Old Trafford.

The match was preceded by a minute's silence in memory of all those who had tragically died in the Bradford City stadium fire one week ago. I am pleased that everyone in the pub honoured their memory by remaining silent for the full minute. When the game kicked off Man Utd seemed nervous, and Everton had by far the best chance of the first half. Fortunately, John Gidman came to our rescue by making a goal line clearance and saving what was almost the opening goal for Everton. The game remained tense during the second half, but I was delighted with every minute that passed by, because it meant that Manchester United were still in the game. My hope was that we could hang on until the last few minutes and then grab a goal that would allow Everton too little time to respond. However, as the game reached the 75- minute mark, disaster struck, when Kevin Moran became the first player to be sent off during a F.A Cup Final.

The pub was initially stunned into silence. Kevin Moran had committed a foul that was worth a booking at most, but referee Peter Willis, possibly sensing the opportunity to make a name for himself, made the decision to send off the visibly shocked player.

"He probably said something to the referee" said an Everton fan, unable to believe his team's good fortune.

"Well, I didn't see him say anything" said Tony angrily.

"He can't have just sent him off for the foul," said the knowledgeable Chris.

"Well, that's the Final ruined", said a visibly deflated Mark.

I however, said nothing. I just stared at the television screen in disbelief. Kevin Moran was clearly in a daze as he walked from the pitch, absolutely shattered by a woeful refereeing decision. Kevin Willis had embarrassed Kevin Moran in front of his watching family and friends and the whole of the footballing world. Eventually, the game re-started, and I felt numb inside as I waited for the Everton onslaught. Initially, I could only hope that my team would hang on for as long as possible, but as the minutes ticked by, I began to think that they could make it through to the final whistle at 0-0. And, by the time that extra time had reached half time without major incident I was dreaming of a replay next week. Surely not? This, after all, was Everton.

Then, remarkably, five minutes into the second half of extra time, I watched transfixed to the screen as Norman Whiteside ran aimlessly with the ball, hopefully eating up more game time. Instead of taking the ball into the corner of the pitch, he cut inside around Pat van Der Hauwe and instantly curled in a low shot beyond the finger- tips of the diving Everton goalkeeper, Neville Southall, into the bottom corner of the net.

I stood up in disbelief and raised both my arms to the ceiling.

"They've fucking scored" I shouted.

Tony grabbed me round the neck in his excitement and wanted to dance, but I pushed him away and sat back down clasping my hands together, as the noise levels in the pub went through the roof. The Manchester United fans jumped up and down, screaming, hugging one another, spilling their drinks and falling over in wild excitement. The noise only began to subside when Mark realised that the game had re-started. The next 10 minutes seemed to last a lifetime. There was nervous laughter and fidgeting from the Man United fans while the Everton fans tried desperately to encourage their team to find an equaliser. I remained motionless, still clasping my hands, while watching the events on the screen unfold. It was difficult to bear the excruciating tension as the ten men of Manchester United hung on bravely. At last, the final whistle was blown and the 1985 F.A Cup final was won. I was able to breathe again for the first time in 15 minutes and I rested my head on the table, feeling completely exhausted. Tony slapped me hard on my back and then pumped his fists.

"Fucking yes" he said, "Let's get the beers in".

The Everton fans went home disappointed while the United fans stayed on cheering and shouting their support, while the F.A Cup was lifted for the second time by Bryan Robson. I felt relief that the game was over and delighted that my team had won. Mark returned from the toilets, where he had been hiding for the past 10 minutes, unable to watch the dying embers of the match.

"I knew we'd win", he said, unconvincingly.

Forty-five minutes later, we were on the bus to Bolton for a night of celebration. I got so drunk that I missed the last bus home to Leigh and had to walk the 12 miles to make it home. As the Leigh town hall clock chimed 4 o'clock, I walked through the deserted town centre and at that moment, I was happy.

Sunday, however, was a write off. I managed to crawl out of bed at lunch time but spent most of the day in an alcoholic stupor. My dad was kind enough to take me back to Salford on the Sunday evening where I went to bed and fell asleep immediately.

I had 3 more days of revision before my first exam on Thursday morning and once more, I was finding it difficult to concentrate. This was different to the brain fog that I had experienced last month because my brain was ready for information input, but I felt fidgety and couldn't settle. I became conflicted as to the true reason behind Bev's delayed return from France. Was she genuinely trying to help me get on with my revision in England or did she have more selfish reasons for remaining in France? It was becoming clear to me that I no longer trusted Bev, but I couldn't determine whether this lack of trust was justified or not. I was managing to get some revision done and progress was being made but I felt that my hyperactivity was starting to have an impact on my flatmates, who all had their own revision to do. With this preying on my mind, I decided that after my first exam on the Thursday morning, I would go back to Leigh for the remainder of my exams and travel into Salford as required. I hoped that I would settle a little in the presence of my parents, while giving my friends the peace they deserved to get on with their work.

Thursday morning meant Micro- Economics, a strong subject for me and a good one to get the ball rolling. The exam went well with most of my favourite subjects being covered and I was sure that I had given a good account of myself. As soon as the exam was over, I didn't hang around to talk to anyone and went straight to the bus stop and headed back home to Leigh. Unfortunately, this was probably the high point of my day because when I arrived in Leigh, I decided to get some lunch and call for a cheeky pint at the Britannia. If there had been no-one that I knew in the pub, I would probably have been fine, but that wasn't the case. Dave and Mick had finished their work on the bins for the day and were well on their way into a 'session'. I joined them for a pint in the Tap Room and quickly turned the subject towards Bev's delayed return from France. To be fair to them, they thought her decision was probably in my best interests and that I should take advantage of the spare time to crack on with my studies. However, my mindset was muddled; I was in self- destruct mode and needed to stew on things a little longer rather than listening to their good advice. Instead of going home after one beer I carried on drinking and the pints started to go down quicker, as the hours passed by. While I was at the bar getting another round in, I spotted Charlie sitting alone in the Lounge.

"Go and see if she can put a smile on your face", said Mick, "but go easy on the self- pity."

It dawned on me that I was being selfish and putting a 'downer' on their evening, so I apologised and went to talk to Charlie.

"Get your coat, you've pulled", I said, smiling.

"Fuck me" she said, "do I look that desperate?"

"Excuse me" I replied, acting hurt by her cutting remark.

She laughed, "Sorry, but I like a bit of muscle on my men."

"That's just steroids", I say, "don't be fooled".

We manage a half -decent conversation and I begin to think that I am sobering up a little. We talk about her latest boyfriend, who sounded very much like her last boyfriend, but this one doesn't hit her. He is out again with his mates tonight and will probably see her for sex later, but he is on a stag do at the weekend, so is unlikely to be around until next week. I tell her that she deserves better, and she smiles and tells me to "fuck off".

There are a group of guys looking over at us who I haven't seen around before. They are all reasonably well dressed but it's hard not to notice that they all have number 1 haircuts, fitted black zipped up jackets, a pair of steel toe-capped boots and union jack badges on their lapels.

"Who are those guys" I ask Charlie.

"Dunno", she says. "They followed me to the bar earlier and cracked a couple of crude remarks, but they seemed more interested in watching Dave and Mick. I don't think they're local.

Charlie asks me how things are going at uni, and I tell her about my exams.

"What, you're in the middle of your exams, and you're out getting pissed, I thought you were supposed to be the clever one?"

"I know", I say, "I need to sort myself out, it's probably best that I get off."

I finish my drink and thank Charlie for her company and head to the toilet. On my way out, Dave and Mick are getting ready to leave, so I follow them out of the back door of the pub. As soon as I step foot onto the pavement, the fresh air hits me, followed by a sharp punch on the side of my head. I turn quickly and take a swing at my assailant. My fist hits home and I hear his nose pop and a spray of blood shoots out in my direction. My fighting prowess is short lived as my feet are kicked from beneath me and I fall to the ground. I look up and see a group of lads surrounding me, just as a steel toe cap connects with my ribs. I try to roll away, but a stamp on my back prevents me from getting too far. Now, in some discomfort, I brace myself for the next impact, but none comes. I begin to struggle to my feet and see Dave and Mick chasing off a couple of lads, while another two are lying on the floor. One is desperately trying to stop the blood from pouring out of his nose and I guess that might be my doing. It is clear from the scene before me, that the fight is already over, and the two remaining guys manage to scuttle off as they see Dave and Mick returning.

Mick flexes his hands while looking carefully at his knuckles and I can see that his lip his bleeding.

"Who the fuck is Sir Oswald Moseley?", he says, staring at a badge torn away from one of the thugs, during the fight.

"He was a British fascist between the 2 World Wars", I say, "why, who were they?"

"Probably the BNP", says Dave. "Fucking racist cunts. They might as well be wearing bloody swastikas."

"What, like the National Front?", I say, shocked by Dave's revelation.

"Yes, same breed", says Dave, "I'm just grateful that you were here to help."

"Yeah right", I say, "I spent all of the fight on the floor; I think you two saved me from a real kicking".

"He means you evened the numbers out, Adam" says Mick.

"And you did put one of them down with that punch, it was a real corker."

I look towards the pub door and see Charlie, standing there.

"You guys alright?", she asks. "I saw them follow you out. Patrick has phoned the police."

"Our cue to leave then", says Dave, "let them know it was four members of the British National Party, not that they will do fuck all about it."

"Ok", says Charlie. She looks me up and down and asks if I want a taxi to take me home. I prefer to get off, so I thank her and begin my hobble towards home.

By the time I make it home the pain was starting to kick in, so I shouted good night to my parents in the living-room and went upstairs to look for some painkillers. Thankfully, my mum and dad were watching something good on television, and both shouted "goodnight," without the need to see their bruised son. I needed to get some sleep and would assess the damage in the morning.

The following morning my ribs ached and the stamp on by back had left a nasty looking bruise. When I finally crawl out of bed, both of my parents are out, so I manage to get some breakfast without facing the third degree. I tread carefully around the house to try and get rid of some of the stiffness in my aching joints. I am soon back upstairs lying on the bed again.

I consider my current predicament. My next exam is on Monday, so I have 3 days to recover from my bumps and bruises and get some revision done. All thoughts of Bev are eliminated from my mind as I focus all my efforts on getting physically and mentally fit for Monday. I decide to take a bath to relax the tightness around my muscles and while this causes some discomfort the warm water does help me to feel better. When I go to the toilet, I notice some blood in my pee and can only hope that it is nothing serious, because I won't be going to the doctors today. My ribs are very sore, and it is highly likely that a couple of them are broken, but I don't think there is much I can do about that, apart from rest. My mum returns home from shopping and I tell her that I am revising, so she makes me a drink and something to eat. I begin to feel a little better after some hot chicken soup and take some more tablets and try to get some revision done. Unfortunately, I fall asleep, and my mum wakes me up and asks about the bruises on my hands and face. I tell her that I fell over while walking through the park drunk, last night, and she calls me "a bloody stupid sod, who should know better at my age".

By Monday I am in much better shape and the blood in my pee is gone. I go into Salford to take my first history exam and return home immediately afterwards to start my revision for my second history exam on Wednesday afternoon. The first exam goes remarkably well but I could have done with more revision time for the second exam on Wednesday. However, I am sure that I have passed both and have no time for regrets, as my fourth exam is on Friday morning, and I need to get out my Economic History books. The European Cup Final between Liverpool and Juventus is on Television tonight and marks the 17th Anniversary to the day since Manchester United beat Benfica 4-1 at Wembley in 1968, to become the first English winners of the European Cup, one year after Celtic had done the same for Scotland. Ian and Nick have gone over to Brussels to watch the game and I said that I would look out for them, but I need to stay in my room and get my head down. My dad pops his head round my bedroom door to let me know that the game has been delayed by stampeding Liverpool fans causing a wall to collapse on the Juventus fans. The match is being played at the Heysel Stadium which has been used previously for the final but looks to have seen better days. I hear later that 39 Juventus fans have died while 600 supporters have been injured, but the game goes ahead, and Juventus win 1-0 with a penalty by Michel Platini. I think about Ian and Nick and hope they are ok.

The blame is being laid firmly with the Liverpool supporters and the following day UEFA allocate responsibility to Liverpool and charge 26 of their fans with manslaughter. I telephone Nick's parents and both he and Ian are fine and on their way home.

On Friday I take my Economic History exam and feel that it went well, so on my way home I call in at my mother's hairdresser and treat myself to a perm on the back of my head. My hair has been getting too long and needs washing every day, so hopefully the perm will keep it in better shape. I sit in the shop window with a plastic bag on my head for the best part of an hour but it's worth it, just to look better than Liverpool's Mark Lawrenson, when I am standing in the heart of the Social Sciences defence.

Later that day, with pressure mounting on the F.A to ban our clubs from European football competitions, Margaret Thatcher sticks her upper-class beak in and tells them to withdraw English clubs from European competition, before they are banned. Consequently, Everton, who have won the League this season after years of Liverpool domination, won't be able to take part in next season's European Cup, while Manchester United will be excluded from the Cup Winner's Cup. While I'm not too disappointed by this news, it must feel like a real kick in the teeth for the Evertonians whose team have been magnificent this season. On a more positive note, Liverpool have failed to win a single trophy this season. Having lost their First Division title to Everton this season they also lost 1-0 to them in August's FA Charity Shield, following a Bruce Grobbelaar own goal. They lost 1-0 to Tottenham Hotspur in the early rounds of the League Cup, a trophy which was eventually won by Norwich City who beat fellow relegated club Sunderland 1-0 in the final. Their 1-0 defeat to Juventus in the European Cup Final comes after a 1-0 defeat against Independiente in the Intercontinental Cup and a 2-0 loss to Juventus in the European Super Cup. Their 2-1 defeat to Manchester United in the semi-final of the F.A Cup was the cherry on the cake for United fans while our 1-0 win at Anfield in the League was also a memorable result. As a Manchester United fan, I need to get my pleasure while I can as I'm sure Liverpool will be back to winning everything again next season.

My final exam takes place on Monday and it's a tough one. Macro Economics is a subject that Nick and Ian are taking this year as part of their Economics course and all three of us meet up before the exam. I ask them about Heysel, but they were at the opposite end of the ground and couldn't make sense of what was happening. They only learned of the terrible events of the night from news bulletins and were as shocked as the rest of us over proceedings. After covering the rights and wrongs of the night's aftermath, Ian became more interested in what I had done to my hair, and I could still see him laughing as we took our seats in the examination hall. The exam was as tough as expected but I was sure that I had done enough to pass, and that was the main target. Nick, on the other hand, walked out of the exam after less than an hour and will need to take it again during the summer. Fortunately, for him, the exam doesn't count towards his final grading as only the 3rd year counts for the pure Economics students.

As I walked out of the examination hall following my final exam, I felt an enormous sense of relief. The last couple of weeks have felt like a living nightmare and I feel exceptionally lucky to have come through them in one piece. I now need to take stock of my life and get back on track, because while progress has been made, I still have more growing up to do.

CHAPTER 11.
HERE COMES THE SUMMER.
June 4th 1985 – July 7th 1985.

I am lying on my bed listening to the radio and on comes 'Here comes the summer' by the brilliant Undertones from 1978, sounding very much like the Ramones.

I am dreaming of the sun on my back, a clear blue sea, golden beaches and Bev in a two -piece bikini. What more could any man want from a summer holiday abroad?

My exams are over, Bev will be back in England on Wednesday, and I have almost 4 months of freedom ahead of me. The excitement building within me wants to burst out and celebrate life to the max, while the anger and disappointment that I felt following Bev's letter in May, is long forgotten. Now, I just want my woman home, to book a holiday in the sunshine and to begin living my best life. What could possibly go wrong?

Even the England cricket team manage to get on board with my optimistic outlook, when they beat Australia by 8 wickets at Lords, in the latest one-day International, with an outstanding knock of

117 not out by Graham Gooch. The series, however, is lost 2-1.

Beverley and I meet at the George and Dragon on Wednesday lunchtime, and once again it is wonderful to see her. She has a lovely tan and is wearing a short and slinky green dress which shows off her amazing long legs. I can't help being overwhelmed by her natural beauty and any concerns that I had over her current feelings for me, are wiped away by her glowing smile. I greet her with an enthusiastic hug that almost crushes her spine, and then devour her sexy brown neck. She giggles and asks if I have missed her.

"Actually" I say sarcastically, "I've been reading an enthralling new book and had forgotten you were coming home, until I saw it on the calendar this morning".

"Is that right, she replies, with a fake snarl, "You can go off people, you know".

I ask what she has been doing with herself over the past few weeks, while I have been slaving over my books. She talks of new girlfriends, relaxing with a glass of wine and sunbathing. There isn't any hint of bad behaviour in her update.

I tell Bev about a function that is taking place at Leigh Cricket club on Saturday, and she asks if she can bring Eileen along for the day. While I would have preferred it to just be the two of us, it will be nice to see Eileen again and I tell Bev that I will pick them both up in my dad's car, and we can walk down to the club from my parents' house. I don't think that Eileen has been seeing anyone since Tony, but Bev says that she does occasionally go out with Elaine and her friends.

With the arrangements made, we have another couple of drinks and talk about all the fantastic places we could go to in the world, on our summer holiday. I am thinking about a Greek or Italian Island while Bev favours the South of France. Our only issue will be getting the money together, but Bev does have some savings and I can earn some cash by helping my dad on the window round. Bev seems happy with life and is relaxed and very attentive and tactile. On the walk back to her house we take a short cut through the remains of some long- abandoned business premises and stop for a snog. We quickly become aroused by the passion of the kiss and the pleasant feeling of having the warm sun on our backs. After 2 months apart the faintest touch of exposed flesh is exhilarating, and we end up making love against the romantic setting of an old factory wall. My ribs are still sore, but the flesh is willing, and the lust is satisfied for both of us at a gentle steady pace that reflects the mood of the warm sultry day. Bev puts her knickers in her handbag, and we walk the rest of the way home with a broad smile on our faces.

Saturday turns out to be a great day for all three of us. The sun is shining, loud pop music is blaring from the marquee and hundreds of people are buzzing around enjoying themselves. We purchase some food from one of the many stalls set out and find our way into the music tent and grab some seats. A punk version of Nelly the elephant is blasting through the huge speakers and a group of younger lads that I recognise from the cricket club are jumping up and down on the dance floor and kicking out their legs to the sound of the music. I go to the bar for the drinks and look back at the girls talking excitedly to one another about what has been going on in their lives. At the bar, I bump into an old school friend called Phil, who plays for Leigh Cricket club as their opening bowler. He is suitably impressed that I am entertaining two ladies and I joke about my sexual appetite being larger than most men's. I'm sure that he doesn't believe me, but it gets a laugh. He tells me that a large screen is going to be erected later to show the Barry McGuigan world title fight against Eusebio Pedrosa.

I return to the girls with our drinks, and we talk about life in Paris, exams, care homes and holidays, while carefully avoiding the subject of religion. Eileen has already booked to go to St Ives with her parents in July while Bev tries to convince me that the South of France is the place to be. I rub my fingers across my aching ribs and think about telling the girls about my adventure outside the Britannia, but it is not a story for today, so I tell them the exciting news about the Barry McGuigan fight instead. It is crazy what a difference a couple of weeks can make, and at this precise moment, I could not be any happier. Is this what people mean when they talk about the ups and downs of love? This time last year I was a moderately happy, semi -normal, functioning human being, whereas now I am an incredibly happy, sometimes sad, emotional wreck.

The three of us do some people watching while Bev and I get increasingly drunk and then we all hit the dance floor when our limbs are feeling sufficiently flexible.

The World Championship Boxing match begins, and Barry McGuigan delivers the fight of his life, winning a unanimous points decision after 15 rounds of blood and guts against a classy opponent. It feels like the perfect end to a perfect day. I order a taxi for the girls and arrange to see Bev for a walk on Sunday. Eileen is giggling as she stumbles into the taxi, and I suspect that she may be a little tipsy.

The following week I go window cleaning with my dad for a couple of days and while the early mornings are a pain in the arse, I view every clean window as a step closer to my summer holiday with Bev, and so it all seems worthwhile.

Unfortunately, everything changes on Wednesday night. While Bev and I are in the Pied Bull having drinks with Tony and Susan, we bump into Scarlett who is single again having split up with her married man. I continue talking to Tony and Susan while Bev talks to Scarlett, and it is obvious from their exchanges that they have something exciting to discuss. The news is that Scarlett and her friends have booked a holiday to the South of France leaving next Thursday, and there is a free place as someone has had to drop out at the last minute. Bev pleads with me to allow her to go but both of us know that she has already made up her mind. I know that the South of France is Bev's dream holiday, and I would probably have succumbed to her will and gone with her choice of destination, when it came to making the final decision. However, it now looks as though that she would sooner go with her girlfriend, rather than her boyfriend. I try hard to hide my disappointment in front of Tony and Susan, but I feel angry inside as Bev knows how much I have been looking forward to getting away with her.

"Of course, you should go", I say, as my heart sinks to the pit of my stomach, "We can go away another time, I say, wanting to throw up my words. 'Road to Nowhere', by the Talking Heads comes on the Jukebox and I look over towards Scarlett and wonder if she has put it on for me.

My evening is ruined, but it is obvious that Bev is beyond excited by developments. I don't know what the lads have planned for the summer, but I now need to find out quickly. Last year the 6 of us hired a boat and went cruising on the Norfolk Broads and while this may sound tame, it ended up being the best holiday I have ever been on. We managed to get ourselves into all kinds of trouble and I don't think that I have ever laughed so much at the insanity of it all. It was the summer of drinking Grolsch with the flip back tops and sun- bathing on the roof of our boat meandering its way down the river. At one point we took a wrong turn and ended up bobbing violently up and down on the North Sea, while being chased by the Police, presumably for our own safety. However, while it was undoubtedly a great holiday, it wasn't one that I had planned on repeating this year.

As it turned out 3 of the lads, had already made their plans and it was left to Mark, Colin and I to sort ourselves out. We meet at the Britannia to discuss our holiday plans on Friday afternoon, but progress is slow, as we are enjoying our pints and don't have any holiday brochures to look at. We make a list of all the things we enjoyed about last year's holiday and come up with being on the water and drinking. This was as far as we'd got, until Patrick's interjection.

"Why don't you go to the Isle of Man, they've got all day drinking laws and you will need to travel over the sea by boat to get there".

Patrick had somehow managed to meet all our criteria with just one suggestion. With the destination agreed, we needed details and once again Patrick was able to help with a brochure. It turned out that accommodation in Douglas was quite cheap and that there was a ship going to the Isle of Man on the 13th July, so we booked it. It's amazing what 3 lads in a pub can achieve when they put their minds to it. As it happens, I have already been to the Isle of Man with my parents when I was nearly 10 in 1974. I remember the World Cup being on the television and England not playing in the Finals as a result of Brian Clough and Jan Tomaszewski, but I couldn't remember much more about the holiday. I suppose I would be looking for a different type of experience now that I had doubled in age.

It's the start of another Ashes series and England beat Australia by 5 wickets in the first Test match at Headingly with a majestic knock of 175 by Tim Robinson from Nottinghamshire.

I feel much happier now that our holiday is booked but I am still pissed off with Bev, who now has some making up to do. Fortunately, Bev is keen to reward me for being such a decent boyfriend and has planned a special treat for me. On arrival at her house on the following Tuesday, I am greeted by her wearing a skimpy cream coloured boob tube, a short shiny black mini-skirt, fish net stockings, high heels, and no underwear. Bev unzips my trousers and goes down on her knees, lubricating me with her tongue. She gazes up at me with her large brown puppy dog eyes and demands that I punish her for being such a bad girl. I pick her up and lie her down on her parents dining room table, pressing myself against her labia and gently massaging an opening inside her with my penis, searching diligently for her clitoris. An involuntary spasm indicates success and Bev makes a high squeaking noise and demands that I go at it hard and fast. I consent to her requirements, and we match each other thrust for thrust, accompanied by rhythmic moaning and lust fuelled swearing. Our sole purpose is to climax fast and together. The dining room table hasn't seen anything like it before and both portions are served simultaneously. She is hot, she is on fire, she is sexy, and she is going on a beach holiday in the South of France without me.

As it happens, I am well acquainted with being apart from Bev and her week in France flies by, as I focus on other things.

The police arrest 13 suspects in connection with last year's Brighton bombing, I read Lord of the Flies and Wimbledon begins its annual fortnight of strawberries and cream. John Lloyd and Jo Durie represent Britain's best hopes of success this year and so we can probably kiss goodbye to the second week of the competition, if we are hoping for National glory. Virginia Wade is still plying her trade 8 years after beating Betty Stove in the Silver Jubilee Final of 1977. I can remember listening to the commentary on the car radio as my parents and I returned home from our summer holiday to Tenby. Sue Barker was also in the semi-finals that year, but she lost to Betty Stove, or it would have been an all British final. I can't imagine that ever coming close to happening again during my life- time, with the way things are going in British tennis. We don't seem to get many working-class kids coming through at the highest level and the posh ones don't really have the heart for a battle when it comes down to it.

Bev returns from her holiday early on Friday morning and we have a night out planned with Tony and Susan on the Saturday. When I arrive at her house on Saturday evening Bev is still in the process of getting ready and seems irritable and snappy. She assures me that all is well, but I can tell there is something troubling her and my instincts are usually right. I give her time to compose herself because she seems to be spoiling for a fight and I don't want us to get the night off to a bad start when we are about to meet up with Tony and Susan. I know I have done nothing to upset Bev and so I can only assume that something has happened today, that I am so far unaware of. No doubt I will find out at some point during the night. I talk to Tony as we make our way to the party, leaving Bev to talk to Susan and hoping that whatever is troubling her, can be quickly resolved. The party is a 'housewarming' being hosted by one of Tony's friends from the bank and it is only on arrival that I realise that it is the blonde-haired, blue-eyed stunner that I met at their Christmas Party in January. Maria welcomes us to her new home and tells us to go through to the kitchen for drinks. Tonight, Maria is wearing a navy-blue, low-cut top showing a tantalising glimpse of her cleavage and a pair of skin-tight jeans, and a pair of high heeled shoes. Maria, once more, looks 'absolutely amazing', but I need to get to the bottom of what is bothering Bev, if we are going to salvage something from the evening. Our conversation is laboured, and Tony and Susan have noticed that Bev is not herself tonight and are wondering what is wrong. Eventually, I have had enough of pandering to her and ask what I have done to warrant tonight's sulking. This only upsets her more and she storms out of the room, leaving me standing there feeling stupid and confused. Maria walks into the room to announce that hot food is now ready in the kitchen, and she notices me standing alone.

"Adam?", she says smiling.

"Yes", I say, feeling a little uncomfortable.

"It's lovely to see you again, I hoped you'd come."

"Thanks for inviting us", I say, "You told me you were looking to buy a house, and you've only gone and done it, well done, it's lovely".

"Thanks", she says, "I'm now the proud owner of a 25 year long Mortgage".

"I'm sure it's worth it", I say, laughing, "How's Jenny, does she like the house?".

"She adores it, she's with her grandparents tonight. Where's your girlfriend?"

"Probably tucking into the food" I say, unconvincingly.

"I'll leave you to join her, nice talking again".

She puts her hand on my shoulder and softly kisses my cheek, and I get a strong whiff of her alluring perfume, as she smiles and glides away. As I stand alone once more, feeling a little giddy by the recent attention, I see Bev standing in the entrance of the doorway and she doesn't look pleased.

The evening becomes a living nightmare for me as I try to maintain the impression that all is well in the world. There are some party games and dancing but Bev refuses to get involved and just sips on her wine and says nothing. I dance with Tony and Susan but feel like a gooseberry and try to avoid eye contact with Maria in case Bev causes a scene. I am bewildered by what is causing Bev to act in this way and embarrassed by her behaviour.

Eventually, it is time to leave, and I give Maria a hug and thank her for a lovely evening. As the four of us ride home in a taxi Bev remains silent and I make small talk with Tony and Susan. Our first port of call is Bev's house and I get out with her and wave off Tony and Susan. Finally, my anger explodes.

"What the fuck is wrong with you tonight"?

"I've met someone else" says Bev, already starting to cry.

The words hit me like a hammer blow and a shiver rips its way through my body.

"His name is Graham, I met him on holiday in France and he's from Liverpool. I went to meet him today and that's why I was late getting ready".

I am crushed. I want to run away, but I'm stuck to the spot, looking dazed and stupid.

"Well, say something", says Bev, sniffing.

"Fuck you", I manage, before finally managing to turn and walk away.

The following day, I refuse to take Bev's calls and remain in my room feeling desperately unhappy. I want to cry but feel that if I start, I may never stop. Tony calls round with Susan but I can't see them either and I remain in my bedroom.

It is Thursday before I agree to talk to Bev, and I arrange to meet her in Pennington Park. That day, a 13-year-old girl called Ruth Lawrence, gets a first-class degree from Oxford University in Mathematics, and I wonder if she has ever had her heart broken.

On my arrival at the park, Bev seems genuinely pleased to see me, which is bizarre considering her behaviour on Saturday. I am determined not to say much, as I have a lot of swear words in my vocabulary and I don't want to use them all at once. She apologises for her behaviour at the party last Saturday and asks that I forgive her for being such a bitch. She now thinks that she might have made a mistake and been hasty in her decision to end our relationship. While part of me would love for this to be true, my major response is one of anger, and I lose my temper.

"You cannot be serious", I say, releasing my inner John McEnroe, "You choose to go on holiday with your friends, sleep with another bloke, but now think you might have made a mistake? Well, woopy fucking doo, lets book our cock-sucking wedding."

"I can't deal with this", I say,

She looks at me, pursing her lips, as though she is about to burst into tears, but says nothing.

"I need time to think as I'm not sure I can cope with this kind of crazy behaviour anymore. Call me on Sunday, and we can talk again". I leave her standing in the park alone and walk home crying.

That weekend Martina Navratilova beats Chris Evert Lloyd 4-6, 6-3, 6-2 in the Women's singles Final at Wimbledon, while a 17-year-old Boris Becker becomes the first unseeded winner of the Men's singles Final, when he beats Kevin Curran 6-3, 6-7, 7-6, 6-4. It is a remarkable achievement for such a young man, and he becomes my first tennis hero since the magnificently charismatic Bjorn Borg hung up his tennis racket at the age of 26 in January 1983. I hope that Boris manages to remain grounded having achieved success at such a young age.

During the men's final Bev does call me as arranged, to tell me that she has changed her mind again and that she has decided to stay with Graham. Quite frankly, I am too exhausted to care anymore and while I do feel desperately sad over the end of my first true love, there is also an element of relief that it is all over. Surely, love wasn't meant to feel like this.?

CHAPTER 12.
THE ISLE OF MAN

July 8th – July 21st 1985.

Over the next few days, I take stock of my 'existence' and think about all the good things that are making me happy in 1985 and adding true value to my life. I have 2 amazing parents that love me, good friends that have my back, a good education, good health, my football team, and my books, and next Saturday I am going on holiday to the Isle of Man. I need to cherish what is important to me, look after and savour it and make good choices as to how I can evolve further.

It is said that experience makes life more meaningful, and I can see that now my relationship with Bev is over. I have experienced love and lost love, but life is about more than one relationship, no matter how good or bad that relationship turns out to be. A person should learn from life's varied experiences and not be afraid of failure, but welcome new opportunities and grow from them. Happiness is nobody's given right, it comes from your actions, so you should strive to be your best person and do your utmost to remain fulfilled while adding value to the world. Just as ripples spread out when a pebble hits the water, the actions of individuals have far- reaching effects, so be brave and the world will become a better place for all. And there ends, my party -political broadcast on behalf of the Dalai Lama.

During the week, England lose the 2nd Test match against the Australians by 4 wickets, largely as a result of Allan Borders first innings knock of 196, and the series is now tied at 1-1. However, with the 3rd Test to begin on Thursday, there is still everything to play for in the series.

Live Aid is also taking place on Saturday and promises to be an unbelievable occasion that will surely go down in history, as one of the greatest music extravaganzas of all time. However, this isn't what it is about. The concert has been organised by Bob Geldof and Midge Ure as a follow up to the Christmas Charity single, 'Do they know it's Christmas' to aid the hundreds of thousands of Africans dying of starvation in Ethiopia. Images of people starving to death have been shown on TV while the western world watches on, no doubt bewildered by the chasm of wealth existing between the world's richest and poorest nations. It is another example of how Capitalism works for some at the expense of others, and it is a sad reflection of our world that while more millionaires are celebrating their vast wealth every year, increasing numbers of the world's population are dying.

I was a massive fan of Bob Geldof and the Boomtown Rats in the late 1970's because of singles like 'Looking after number one' and 'Mary of the 4th

form' and think that what he has achieved is amazing. He can be arrogant and sanctimonious at times, but he is another of those 'special breed of people' that 'get things done'. He can bully, cajole and inspire people in equal measures until he gets his own way, and to convince so many stars with massive egos to perform for free is a Churchilian accomplishment.

As Mark, Colin and I make our way to the Isle of Man by Car, Train and Ship, the most iconic music event in history is kicking off at Wembley stadium in London, John F Kennedy stadium in Philadelphia and numerous other locations across the world. Status Quo are the first band to play at Wembley as the music begins at Midday with the appropriately named 'Rockin all over the World' hit record quickly getting the crowd jumping. An estimated 1.9 billion people will be watching the live broadcast which is almost 40% of the world population.

Unfortunately, we missed most of the event due to our travels, and by the time we arrived at our accommodation in Douglas, Isle of Man, only the acts from Philadelphia were still to be broadcast on the TV. It seemed unfair that Phil Collins had managed to fly from London to Philadelphia, playing badly at both events, while we couldn't manage to locate a fucking TV anywhere on the ship to watch it.

By Sunday, Queen are being hailed by the newspapers and TV as the greatest rock band in the world while some of the biggest pop bands of the day have proven that they can't perform live. Adam Ant, Nik Kershaw, The Thompson Twins and Duran

Duran all showed themselves up for what they are while Led Zep revealed why they had packed it all in years ago.

The Isle of Man became separated from Great Britain and Ireland by 6500 B.C and since 1866 has been a Crown dependency with a democratic self-government. In between, it had been attacked by the Viking and Norse Kingdoms and owned by the English and the Scots.

As England captain, David Gower, is accumulating 166 runs against the Australians in the 3rd Ashes test, the 3 of us go out in Douglas on an all- day bender. As afternoon passes to evening time and Colin is emptying the contents of his stomach so that he can continue drinking, I meet the wonderful Evelyn from County Galway, in the Republic of Ireland. At 25, she is older than me and is holidaying in the Isle of Man with her 2 younger cousins who are both 18. She has long black hair, brown eyes and is exceptionally pretty. Evelyn has a gorgeous smile, a hearty laugh and a wonderful Southern Irish twang, not shared by the girls in the North of Ireland. She works at a furniture business in Galway and has a relaxed easy- going approach to life, which is refreshing. I ask Evelyn to guess what she thinks that I do back in England, and she thinks I might be a bus conductor. I take a moment to ponder over the 1970's sitcom 'On the Buses' starring Reg Varney and Bob Grant but can't see me in the guise of Stan or Jack. She does have a strange sense of humour, so she might be joking with me, but I couldn't say for sure.

Evelyn has hired a car for the week and over the next few days takes me to Douglas Head Lighthouse made by brothers David and Thomas Stevenson in 1857, the Laxey Wheel built in 1854 to pump water from the surrounding area and revolving at approximately three revolutions a minute, Port Erin, which is a seaside village in the South West of the island, and the Fairy Bridge where we remember to wish the fairies Good Morning as we pass by. The Fairy Bridge is one thing I do recall from my last visit to the island in 1974.

The Isle of Man is also famous for the Tourist Trophy, Time Trial races, which are an annual motorcycle racing event which has been run on the island since 1907, in May or June. The event is known to be the most dangerous racing event in the world and Mark would have loved it if we had been able to watch this year's Formula one event. It was won by Joey Dunlop from Northern Ireland on a Rothmans Honda, in 1 hour, 59 minutes and 12 seconds. Dunlop also won the Junior TT event and the Senior TT event giving him a hat trick of wins this year and he is destined to become a true legend of the event.

On Tuesday night Evelyn and I go to a nightclub in Douglas and take along her cousins. We dance the night away and share a kiss or two while chatting about our lives. There is some trouble outside the club and one man is left bleeding and unconscious on the pavement, after being punched from behind by a coward in a tracksuit. I go back into the club to look for Evelyn's cousins, but I find them safe and well and they seem more excited than scared about the unrest. That night, Evelyn and I talk for hours about our lives and end up falling asleep in her car, holding hands. There is frolicking and fondling and plenty of hot passion that results in the car windows getting steamed up, but I feel that there may be someone back in Galway, waiting patiently for Evelyn's return. However, our brief encounter ends up being the perfect holiday romance as we talk endlessly, make each other laugh and thoroughly enjoy one another's company. Evelyn is going back to Ireland on Thursday morning, and there is no time to build a relationship, but the time we spend together is just what I needed after the trauma of the last few weeks with Bev. We agree that there is little merit in keeping in touch, but Evelyn gives me a small silver cross to remind me of our time together in the Isle of Man.

England draw the 3rd Test match with the Australians and the series remains tied at 1-1 with the 4th test due to be played at Old Trafford, Manchester.

On Thursday afternoon with Evelyn on her way back to Ireland, Mark, Colin and I decide to rent some kayaks for the sea. The weather is freezing cold, and it is notable that no-one, not even the crabs have ventured on to the beach today. We take our first nervous steps into the sea and the water is icy and bites our toes and turns our ankles pink. However, once we have capsized a few times, we seem to get over the cold and manage to enjoy ourselves racing up and down the waves. The sea possesses therapeutic qualities which would work wonders on all our sporting injuries, if we had any, but it certainly wakes us up, and by mid- afternoon we are fully invigorated and ready for a few pints in a warm pub. After a few tasty beers we have a Chinese meal back at the flat and arrange to go back to the nightclub tonight. I go for a lie down for a few hours, having had very little sleep during the holiday so far. I am woken up by a young blond girl stealing coins from my bedside table. She isn't a particularly good thief, because she is very loud and gobby and can't stand still for a minute. There are a group of girls staying in the flat above us, so I can only assume that she is with them. She tells me that she is running out of money and asks if she can take some of mine from the table. When I ask her to leave, she offers me a deal.

"Arr, don't be tight, I'll give yer a hand job for a tenner", she says, comically.

I politely refuse her kind offer but tell her she can take some of the coins if she leaves the notes where they are. She seems young and daft and can only be 18, at the most, so I feel a bit sorry for her. I'm sure she could only have left with about £6 but she seems resourceful and will probably make it last.

That night at the club we bumped into the girls from the flat above and I had a bit of a dance with the blond girl and bought her a drink, but we didn't take it any further. Due to my day trips with Evelyn over the past three days, I hadn't spent enough time with Mark and Colin, and so we made up for it with a healthy session of beer and vodka chasers while sitting at the nightclubs long mahogany bar. We sang along to a couple of songs that will always remind me of our holiday in the Isle of Man, largely because of the number of times that they were played. Frankie, by Sister Sledge and Life is Life, by Opus, were played in every pub we went into during the week, and while they wouldn't usually be our kind of music, they are a couple of cracking summer songs to sing along to. If only the sun had made an appearance during our week in the Isle of Man, it could have been mistaken for Benidorm. It was only on the last day of our holiday that Colin told me that the Opus song was called 'Live is Life' but to me it will always be 'Life is Life'. Brrr.

The holiday was over in a flash and as I stood on the ship deck watching the Isle of Man disappear into the distance, we were on our way back to Leigh. The time spent with Evelyn had done me a power of good and I now felt stronger and more able to move forward in my life without Bev. The pedestal on which I had held Bev has been shattered and I now realise that she was far from being the mature and rounded individual that I first thought. In fact, I was beginning to wonder whether I was the mature one during our relationship. I had learned a few things about myself over the past year and while I know that I need to rid myself of my destructive streak and start to become more open with my feelings, I have realised that I am resilient and capable of bouncing back quickly from setbacks.

When we arrive home, I watch a little of the Open Championship Golf at Royal St George's Club in Sandwich. I'm not really a big fan of golf, particularly the watching of it on television, but it is good to see Sandy Lyle win his first title by beating Payne Stewart by one stroke on the final day run in.

CHAPTER 13.
"A LITTLE BIT OF WHAT YOU FANCY."

July 21st- August 31st, 1985.

On my return from holiday, I start to read a book that I have been meaning to read for a long time and while some people have been disappointed with the book, I wasn't. It took me 2 days to read Catcher in the Rye, by J.D Salinger, the book that Mark Chapman was carrying when he shot John Lennon to death, in December 1980. I can't categorically say whether the book influenced Mark Chapman to shoot John Lennon, but it is more likely that he was just a fucking psychopath who wanted to kill someone famous. By doing so, he knew that he would go down in history for what he had done. There was some discussion as to whether Mark Chapman identified with Holden Caulfield and saw Lennon as a fake or a phoney, in accordance with one of the books major themes, but I wouldn't think that he possessed the intellect. Mark Chapman wanted to be famous, but he didn't have any of the necessary attributes to achieve fame in his own right, so he shot a man who was easily accessible to him and had been kind to him that very morning. John Lennon, like anyone else, had his faults, but many of us saw him as a genius and a true working- class hero. He still had a great deal to offer the world in terms of his music and did not deserve to die.

As for the book, I loved it. I think I can understand why it made such an impact in the United States when it was released into the drastically changing world of the 1950's, but I enjoyed it because of the way it impacted me. While I do not profess to have the intellect of Holden Caulfield and no longer believe that I am about to spiral into madness, I do share some of his thoughts about people and society in general. I strongly believe that our world has been built upon the foundations of lies and deceit, and that a large proportion of people that make it to the top of their chosen profession or vocation, are likely to be the biggest liars and cheaters of all. There are exceptions of course, but not as many as one would like to think. Politicians are probably the easiest group of people to pick on, when I say that I don't trust a single one of them. When they say that they got into politics to serve people, I want to puke. They go into politics for the influence it gives them, and to serve their own selfish interests. To be successful in a world built on lies and deceit, it helps your chances if you are prepared to bend a few rules that would question the average person's ethical moral code. However, you do need to stick to the 'rules of the game', and one of the most important rules is 'don't get caught'. For this to work, you need to be clever and manipulative and slimy, and once more I cannot help but think of today's politicians. To play the game, you do not need to be a politician, but as the game was invented a long time ago, it helps if you are one of the select group of people who are 'entitled' or 'born into it'. It is possible to be born into poverty and to learn the game, but then you must be more ruthless than ever, and you must cut off all ties with the person that you used to be.

Holden Caulfield sees the world of the fakes and the phoneys and despises what he sees. I take a moment to consider which of my friends will become the fake or the phoney of the future and sincerely hope that person will not be me. All that I do know at this juncture is that it won't be Mark. Holden believes that people have lost that sense of innocence in the world, apart from his younger sister whose mind has not yet been poisoned. I think back to my younger innocent years and the loving, trustworthy people that I had around me and compare it to what I have observed over the past 6 years, and I am shocked and saddened by what I have learned. I, like Holden, don't want to become part of their world, but sadly, he descends into madness before finding a solution to his angst. I would prefer to develop my own individual meaning to what life has to offer and would like to be measured on how I achieve success as opposed to the success I achieve. I don't want to be defined by my career or my religion, although I accept that I will need to play by society's rules to some extent, to ensure that I have the means to do the things I want in life. However, whatever I go on to do in this world I will always consider myself to be working-class. I have important choices to make and refuse to turn into a grubby, greedy, corrupt, self-obsessed psychopath that manipulates the world and cares little for the 'ordinary man'. Their world is all about power and money and more importantly about maintaining that power and money, so do not expect to share in their good fortune. From a young age, we are preached at by parents, priests, teachers, politicians, employers, the press, TV and the media, who tell you what society expects from you. You probably don't think you take it all on board, but you do. You may not think that you accept their lies, but these people can be very clever, and they assume that you are not. Many of you will believe what they have to say and many of you will learn to repeat what they have to say, and those of you that don't will never change them, because their voice has been well established over hundreds of years. We may not be living in George Orwell's 'Big Brother', 'Totalitarian state,' but every institution in the U.K has been established long ago to keep us in our place, and eventually you will come to realise that it is a case of do as I say and not as I do. In our politics we continue to vote for ego maniacs without scruples, despite being lied to time and time again, when it is obvious that they have no wish to make the world a better place. When they are finally found out, they will talk about lessons learned and then hope you have forgotten all about their lapse when they make the same 'mistake' again, years later. They are arrogant, don't believe that consequences are intended for them and know that they can still rely on your vote if they are prepared to knock a penny off the price of beer every now and again.

Maybe I am a little paranoid or bat shit crazy, because if my friends feel the same way as I do, they aren't telling me. This probably explains why I can sometimes feel a little isolated with my views and opinions. I wonder whether they are oblivious to what is going on in the world or whether they just don't care, but I try not to let this bother me anymore. However, by taking my values seriously, I can sometimes become too concerned with issues like class inequality, gender inequality, sexual and racial discrimination and can often see through the bad intentions, motivations and desires of other people. Sadly, little is changing for the better in our society, despite the occasional lip service by our politicians to such issues. Thirty-nine years have passed by since the end of World War 2 to the start of my story and the problems of the world remain the same, because rich entitled people don't change. Are we still going to be talking about war with the Soviet Union, terrorism, world poverty, climate change, religious intolerance, and social inequalities in another 39 years when it will be 2023? What needs to happen to force the leaders in our world to wake up and for people to become more self-aware. Fortunately, I am finally beginning to appreciate my own feelings, fears and motivations about life and am learning to fit into a harsh society without compromising myself and my principles. I have made good progress in piecing together my own 'meaning of life' in order to make sense out of a world that has no meaning. It is a work in progress and will evolve over time, but it already covers what I want to get out of life and more importantly the behaviours and principles I intend to follow to be successful.

On Sunday 28th July, a walk for AIDs is held in the United States that generates some interest in the news, but I get the feeling that suppression of news on AIDs is still the preferred choice. I am starting to believe that this disease is far more significant and dangerous than is currently being represented by the media. I discuss my thoughts with Tony over a few beers, but he doesn't seem particularly concerned. In fact, he is a little dismissive of it impacting the 'straight man,' while the 'puff's' can go and sort themselves out. I've known Tony long enough to understand that he is full of 'bluff and bluster', but it is obvious that he doesn't yet see AID's, as a major issue for society in general.

Sunny August bursts into view and the 4th Test match against Australia is drawn at Old Trafford, leaving the series stuck at 1-1 with two to play. Mike Gatting scores 160 but it's all in vain, as it doesn't influence the result.

Murder is on the news again, with reports of an incident currently being referred to as the 'White House farm murders'. One of the family members called Jeremy Bamber is interviewed about the killings but he doesn't seem overly bothered about the whole sordid affair. It must be a posh boy thing, because I would be a bit more upset if all my family had just been brutally murdered by someone.

To focus on something more cheerful, I decide to spend some more time on reading another great book and choose 'A Tale of 2 Cities' by Charles Dickens. I've previously read three books by Charles Dickens, including 'Great Expectations' which is considered by many critics to be his 'Magnum Opus,' but I preferred this novel. I think I appreciate it more because it is a historical novel set in London and Paris before and during the French Revolution and as you will know by now, I do love my history. It also has one of the most famous opening sentences in literature but I'm not Charles Dickens so you will have to look it up for yourself.

On Saturday, Mark and I travel to Wembley with Chris to watch Manchester United play Everton in the Charity Shield, which is League winners against Cup Winners and a repeat of the F.A Cup Final played in May. Mark and I have a strong feeling that following the FA Cup win in May, Manchester United could have a real chance at winning the First Division title, this year. Unfortunately, the day is destined for disappointment when we have a couple of major incidents with Chris' car, resulting in a tyre blow out on the way to London and a total engine failure on the way home. In addition, Manchester United fail to show the same level of passion and commitment as they had in May and lose a drab encounter by 2-0. To make matters even worse, we only arrive back in Leigh for a couple of pints before last orders and there is no lock-in tonight. On the plus side, however, I bump into Elaine on the way home, and we arrange a game of tennis for the following Wednesday.

On Tuesday, the first U.K Heart and Lung transplant takes place in Middlesex. The recipient is a three-year-old boy from Dublin, who becomes the world's youngest patient. His condition is described as satisfactory.

I meet with Elaine at the entrance to Pennington Park on Wednesday evening and she arrives sporting a bright lime green tee shirt and a pair of sparkling white shorts. Her legs are tanned and shapely and she looks amazing. We play a few sets of tennis to get the adrenalin flowing, and then decide to get changed and go for a few drinks instead. It is a lovely evening, as we make our way to the Bridgewater Arms and the conversation, much like the adrenalin, is flowing. Elaine and I have much in common and talk about the people we both know, the books we have read, the music we like and the holidays we would like to go on. We are completely at ease in each other's company, and we share a similar sense of humour, if the laughter is anything to go by. As the drinks go down, the laughter turns to flirting and the conversation becomes more personal. By closing time, I am beginning to see Elaine in a more romantic light. I walk her home and we kiss to round off a lovely evening, but the spark isn't there for me and we part without making plans for another date. It all seems a little unfair as Elaine is pretty, clever and funny and I have more in common with her than Beverley, but the X factor is missing and there is nothing I can do about that. I find out that evening that the Sinclair CV has ceased production and I reluctantly cross it off my Christmas list.

The remainder of the month is largely devoted to playing and watching sport because the weather is gorgeous. I play five-a-side football with Chris, tennis with Tony and Crown green bowls with Mark, Colin and Paul. Mark and I also go to Old Trafford to watch Manchester United kick off the 1985-86 season. As September is going to be a busy month for parties, I cut back a little on the alcohol consumption and try to get a bit fitter. Manchester United start off the season with a 4-0 victory over Aston Villa and play exceptionally well, but we have been here before, so I'm not getting over excited just yet. However, a 1-0 win at Ipswich Town, a 2-1 victory at Arsenal and a 2-0 win at home to West Ham United means 4 wins out of 4 and Mark and I can begin to dream.

The England cricket team also performs well in the last 2 tests of the summer and comfortably win the 5th test at Edgbaston, by an Innings and 118 runs. David Gower stars with the bat scoring 215, while swing bowler, Richard Ellison, performs with the ball, claiming match figures of 10/104. England then complete a 3-1 series victory over Australia, and the Ashes is reclaimed after losing 2-1 in Australia in 1982-3, with an Innings and 94 run- success at the Oval. This time it is Graham Gooch that stars with the bat, scoring 196 runs, while Ellison again does the trick with the ball, with second Innings figures of 5/46.

On Saturday, 31st August, Mark and I travel to Liverpool to attend Ian's 21st birthday party at the Territorial Army club. On arrival we are pleased to find out from Ian that Manchester United have completed their 5th consecutive League victory with an impressive 3-1 away win at Brian Clough's Nottingham Forest. We are surprised to learn that one of our goals was scored by former Man City legend Peter Barnes. It always seemed like a strange signing to me, but I won't be complaining if he scores a few more goals this season. When we arrive at the venue, Richard and Ron are sitting at a table near the bar with Jan, who is now very much a part of Ian's life. Nick turns up later in buoyant mood after passing his Macro-Economics re-sit. The seven of us settle down and catch up on the events of the summer, so far. As the room begins to fill up the D.J kicks off proceedings with 'Life is Life' by Opus and I exchange a smile with Mark, as we think back to the Isle of Man. When Mark and Nick go to the bar for more drinks, I decide to ask the D.J to play a Smiths song, which he agrees to do, immediately. On comes 'This Charming Man' with Johnny Marr's familiar guitar riff and Morrissey vocalising his concern over having nothing to wear. There is no-one on the dance floor yet, but I have asked for the song, and I need to give it my support. I walk confidently onto the dance floor and try to give my best impression of Morrissey uncomfortably swaying left and right, without the addition of shrubbery in my back pocket.

I feel good about myself tonight, dressed in my Hawaiian shirt, stonewashed denim jeans (not high waist) and my new pair of white sneakers and am looking forward to a fantastic night out with good friends. The Smith's song is followed by 'She sells Sanctuary' by the Cult, so I remain dancing for a little longer. After performing solo for most of the party guests who have now arrived, I see a group of girls sitting at a nearby table, and with my confidence high, decide to go and talk to them. They immediately start to take the piss out of my accent, comparing it to Vera Duckworth's from Coronation Street, which is a bit harsh. However, they are only messing, because it cannot be any worse than their strong Liverpudlian Brookside twang. After a few laughs I agree to get some drinks and ask an extremely pretty girl called Lucy to help me. She is wearing a black dress with tassels that reminds me of a Charleston dress from the 1920's and her long silver earrings suit her attire perfectly. If she had only worn a matching head band and feather, I could have whisked her back to the jazz age for a dance. The 1920's has got to be one of the most glamorous and exciting eras of the 20th Century and if I owned a Time machine, it is one of the first 'time eras' I would visit. Lucy follows me obediently to the bar where we chat about who we both know at the party. She is tall, blond and slim, which sounds like my type, so we take back our drinks and go for a dance. It has been an exceptionally good year for Madonna, and we dance to her latest song called 'Get into the Groove,' which we try to do, before I take Lucy back to my table and introduce her to my friends.

We are soon dancing again to 'In between Days' by the Cure and 'I'm on Fire' by Bruce Springsteen. We end up kissing on the dance floor, which is lovely and sweet, but she is shy and doesn't have a great deal to say for herself. I am keen to spend time with my friends tonight, but Lucy seems to prefer it when it is just the two of us. She likes to listen to my opinions on music and the government and finds me funny and clever. I don't want to upset her feelings and I encourage her to bring some of her friends over to our table, so that we can carry on the conversation as a group. Lucy seems happy enough with this but clings onto my hand tightly and won't let go, which feels a little restrictive when I want to drink and scratch my nose at the same time. As the party atmosphere goes up another level everyone gets up onto the dance floor and we have a great time fooling around and singing along to the tunes.

Richard happens to mention that Lucy was following me around like a lost puppy, adding that, "I think she really likes you, Adam". It was only then that I realised how badly I was behaving with Lucy. I had initiated the two of us getting together and now I was acting as though I wasn't really bothered about her or her feelings. I do not want to be that kind of person and am angry with myself for behaving like an arsehole. I shouldn't be toying with other people's affections when I clearly hadn't got Bev out of my system. Tonight, should have been about re-connecting with my friends rather than trying to prove something to myself, and I was disappointed with my actions. I felt uneasy about myself because there can be a fine line between confidence and arrogance and it's a trap that far more illustrious people than me have fallen into.

As the evening came to an end, I thanked Lucy for a wonderful night, trying not to appear condescending, and told her what a special beautiful young woman she was. She kissed me and said that it was nice to meet me, and then she was gone. I thought about my liaison with the lovely Lucy for the next couple of days and I knew that I had been in danger of appearing like a heartless tool. She had been the 3rd girl I had been romantically close to in the space of 7 weeks, and while a little of what you fancy does you good, it doesn't necessarily mean that its right for you. Another relationship probably wasn't what I needed at this point in my life, and I needed to relax and enjoy life for everything it had to offer. Bev had managed to rock my foundations and I needed time for some rebuilding work.

CHAPTER 14.
'THE ULTIMATE QUESTION OF LIFE'.

September 1st-October 6th1985.

On Sunday, I read Ernest Hemingway's, 'Old Man and the Sea' which is a short story that resulted in Hemingway winning the Pulitzer Prize in May 1952 and the Nobel Prize for Literature in October 1954. It is a well- written story, without being the most exciting of tales, unless you have some morbid interest in fishing.

But we are now entering the month of September and I have more important matters to consider. With expectant friends and relatives seeking clarification, I still have the tiny matter of deciding what I am going to do for my 21st Birthday party. The discussions and suggestions have dragged on for so long now that Mark is referring to my final decision as 'the ultimate question of life,' and has suggested that I turn to 'Douglas Adams' for the answer. So, with Marks help, I have finally decided to go with two 21st parties because, as Douglas Adams will tell you, 21 x 2 = 42 = the ultimate answer to the ultimate question of life.

To be honest, 'the Hitchhikers Guide to the Galaxy' is one of Mark's favourite books, rather than mine, but I like the concept, and I am happy with the idea of having a party on the two weekends either side of my birthday. My birthday is on a Monday this year, which will also mark the 8th anniversary of the death of Marc Bolan of T. Rex fame, who sadly died when his girlfriend drove her Mini into a tree, with him relaxing in the passenger seat. He was my first musical hero as a child, and as a young boy I can still remember buying the singles Metal Guru and 20th Century Boy from Leigh's Rumbelows store with my saved-up pocket money. I was devastated when I heard that he had died on what was my 13th Birthday.

As for Douglas Adams, I'm not sure why he chose the number 42 to represent the ultimate answer to the ultimate question of life. It didn't do much for Elvis Presley's prospects, as he died on the 16th of August 1977 at the age of 42, while he was sitting on the toilet. And so, with the decision finally made, I will now focus on making up some mix tapes of all my favourite music, so that I can wow my friends and family with my amazing musical taste.

In the news, Jeremy Bamber, (the laid- back posh boy) is arrested, released and re-arrested for the White House Farm murders. I of course, knew that it was him all along.

Jock Stein, Celtic Manager at the time of their 1967 European Cup success, collapses and dies during Scotland's World Cup qualifier with Wales. On the same night England draw with Romania to secure qualification for next year's World Cup.

The second Handsworth riots take place in Birmingham between 9th-11th September where hundreds of people attack the police and property. Handsworth has been predominantly populated by the Black and Asian communities for around 30 years and has one of the highest unemployment rates in Birmingham.

17 years after Enoch Powell's famous 'Rivers of Blood' speech in Birmingham on 20th April 1968 his words reverberate across the media, in a blatant attempt to further stir things up in Handsworth. In his 1968 speech Enoch Powell had strongly criticised mass immigration, especially from the Commonwealth, warning of the potential consequences for the future security of the UK. Powell was sacked from the Conservative party shadow cabinet by Edward Heath the day after his speech and the Race Relations Act was introduced the same year. The Act made it illegal to refuse housing, employment, or public services to a person on the grounds of colour, race, ethnic or national origins. However, it was criticised for poorly translating the new standards of behaviour that were required and little progress has been made regarding ongoing acts of discrimination.

In other news, Ronald Reagan and Elizabeth Taylor both reference the impact that the AIDs epidemic is starting to have across the world, and at last it looks as though the disease is beginning to be taken seriously.

I'm still taking it easy on the alcohol consumption, but I notice blood in my pee again and this time the flow is heavier. I'm unsure as to the cause of the blood as the pain from my 'arse kicking' has long gone. However, I'm suspecting that it could be a sign that one of my kidneys has been damaged, so I will need to be keep a close eye on my water works.

While shopping in town on Wednesday, I bump into Elaine and invite her and her friends to the second of my 21st birthday parties, to be held at the Britannia Pub on the 21st day of September. I haven't seen much of Elaine since we shared a kiss together last month, but I don't think that any awkwardness remains, and I would be upset if it ruined our friendship in any way. I think Elaine realises that I'm not in the right 'head space' to be in another relationship just now.

My first party on the 14th of September is to be a gentler affair with my relatives, but that doesn't mean boring. My dad and his friend Bill build a makeshift extension onto the back of the house, so that more people can fit into the living-room. It reminds me of one of the dens we used to build as kids, and it looks very cool when it is all lit up. Some delicious food is prepared by my mother for the party, an enormous supply of booze is shipped in and my music taste for the evening is of course, amazing. All my aunts and uncles and cousins are in attendance, and all know how to celebrate. There is no such thing as a formal occasion when the family get together and the dancing starts as soon as the music begins, with everyone ready to party. My Aunty Joyce has her own special dance, which is like the Māori Haka but with more energy and facial expressions. It doesn't really compliment my Smiths records, but it is very entertaining to watch and should be used by our rugby guys to intimidate the Kiwis. When some of the relatives are starting to flag, my friends turn up after the pubs have closed and add life back into the proceedings. The evening is a great success and I fully appreciate the effort that everyone has made. One slight downer on the day was a birthday card arriving from Beverley, but I try not to put too much emphasis on her reason for sending the card and manage to compartmentalize it away in my mind. On this occasion, I talk to my mum about the stress that the card had caused me and manage to get one or two things off my chest, rather than bottling things up as per usual. My mum is sensitive to my pain, calm and patient and a very good listener. I am making progress.

One week later and the day of my second party arrives and my friends start to turn up throughout the day. Mark and Colin are with me from lunchtime when we begin proceedings with a couple of pints at the Britannia.

Colin raises his pint and says:

"Til death us do Party."

"Very good", I say, "I like it",

"I'm not just a handsome fucker", Colin says modestly.

"No, no you're not", says Mark.

Chris is the next to arrive, closely followed by Paul.

"No Desmond today, I'm afraid, Adam", says Paul, taking a swig of his beer.

"Who the fucking hell is Desmond", shouts Colin.

"Teabag", says Paul looking confused.

"What the fuck?" "You're only telling me now that the 'brick shit house' is called Desmond?" "You've got to be fucking kidding me?"

"What, you didn't know that Teabag's a Desmond", says Paul, laughing.

"Will you stop fucking saying Desmond, its creeping me out" says Colin, standing up. "I can't process this; I'm going to need to go for a shit now".

We all watch Colin has he makes his way to the toilets and take another gulp of our beer.

"I think Desmond is a great name", says Mark wistfully, 'I think it's Irish'. "Yes, I'm sure its Irish", says Mark.

An hour later, Mike, the Christian, turns up on his bike from Cheshire, while John arrives on the coach from Wolverhampton. Tony and Susan have had a couple of cocktails at the Tropics and arrive in good spirits. Nick and Ian are watching the Liverpool v Everton Derby and are the last to arrive when the party is already underway. I give my music recordings to Patrick to play throughout the course of the evening, while my parents have kindly paid him to prepare a buffet for later in the night. All the girls turn up, including Bev's friend Eileen, which is a nice surprise. To make her feel at home I ask Patrick to play 'Come on Eileen' by Dexys Midnight Runners, and all the lads join in with the chorus.

While she does find our rendition amusing, she ends up blushing, and no matter how much I try to convince her, I can't get her up to dance. There are a lot of brightly coloured, shoulder padded jackets and matching skirts being worn by the ladies tonight, which puts the lads to shame, as they are mostly in their comfortable jeans and tee shirts. Charlie pops over with a pint of lager for my birthday, wearing a pink body suit with extra tassels. The outfit is tight and doesn't leave much to the imagination and not surprisingly turns a few heads, but she is going out with her fella to a club in Manchester tonight and wants to look her best. The Lounge side of the pub has been cordoned off for the party, but it doesn't stop the regulars coming in for a dance and a chat and Dave and Mick both buy me a pint. At one stage in the evening there are 6 pints of lager waiting for me to drink, but I pace myself by drinking faster and spill the rest on the dance floor. My mum and dad arrive later in the night, my mum armed with a camera to record the drunken antics of her only child celebrating his 21st birthday. At some point there is a speech, intending to thank everyone for coming, but more likely to have been made up of nonsensical expletives and comical slurring. Mike is once more the star of the dance floor, energetically 'strutting his stuff' dancing with my friend Yvonne, before leaving at about 11 o'clock for his bike ride back to Cheshire. After drinking enough beer to intoxicate Oliver Reed about a dozen of us stagger back to my parents house to carry on the drinking, but it isn't long before the lads start to fall asleep and it's time to call it a night. Before going off to bed, I make one final attempt at alcohol poisoning, by taking a long drink from a bottle of vodka that Colin has brought along, but my mum takes it away from me and tells me not to be so bloody stupid. She does have a point, but I have- to smile, when I am woken up a couple of hours later by the noise of my dad throwing up in the bathroom. He had been drinking cider all night with his friend Bill and obviously can't handle his drink anymore. That said, Bill can probably drink most of the lads under the table, so I can't blame him for being sick. The following morning, the living room looks like a bomb site, with drunken lads lying all over the floor in between dozens of empty cans of beer. Everyone agrees that it was a 'belting do' and that's all that matters. Mark and Colin are the last to leave just as they were the first to arrive yesterday and I arrange to meet them for a quiet pint at the Britannia later this evening.

During the month of September, Manchester United have been on a roll, and after winning their next 3 games by a 3-0 score, they follow this up with a 5-1 victory at West Bromwich Albion. Their 10th game of the season ends in a 1-0 win over Southampton, which means 10/10 so far, which is a magnificent accomplishment for the Red Devils. Could this finally be the year that Manchester United win the League again after 17 years of failure. Only time will tell.

Back in June, the 4 months of freedom lying ahead of me had seemed like it would last forever, but with only one week left of my holiday, I am left wondering where all the time went. I have also booked myself on a Careers course for a week, which seemed like a good idea at the time. The course has been arranged for 3rd year students looking to break into the job market at the end of their final year at university. It should prove to be a useful indicator of what the job market might be like in the summer of 1986, and I do need to start considering my future career. I have decided that I have had enough of examinations and the student lifestyle and need to start earning myself some proper money by getting a decent job next year. There will be a variety of potential employers at the event, so there will be lots of opportunities to demonstrate competencies and learn a few more skills during the week. I have been informed that there will be more than 100 students at the event with everything being done on site, including accommodation and a bar, so I am anticipating a few extra curricula activities taking place during the evenings.

I enjoy testing my brain and some of the exercises are challenging, but lots of fun. We are split into groups of 6 and will get the opportunity to complete all the different exercises, during the week. One person in the group is instructed to take the lead in each of the exercises, giving everyone the chance to demonstrate their leadership skills on at least a couple of occasions. I am to be the leader of the first task of the day which involves me going to see an 'object' in the adjacent room, before returning to my team and describing the object to them. The idea is to replicate this object in the function room which turns out to be a statue made up of Lego. After my description of the object, the other members of my team are required to take turns in going to view it, for which they have been allocated responsibility for replicating a part of the statue. As leader, I initially entered the other room with no idea what to expect and went with an open mind. The Lego statue is made up of different shapes and different colours of Lego and I need to quickly formulate a plan as to how the team can rebuild the object in the function room. I have only a limited time with the object and cannot touch it. As I can't possibly remember everything about the statue, I break it down in my mind from top to bottom and nominate the 5 members of my team to remember different parts of the structure. When I return to the function room, I describe the whole of the structure and give instructions on what I expect each of the team to recall when they enter the room. Fortunately, the exercise goes well, and we accurately build the structure with the Lego blocks provided. We are one of the groups to successfully complete the task, so we are off to a good start.

Our team is made up of 3 boys and 3 girls from a couple of the Manchester Universities. The other 2 lads are from Salford and are called Andy and Simon, but they are on science courses, and I haven't seen them before. A girl called Karen is also from Salford and I have seen her on a couple of occasions at Castle Irwell. The remaining 2 girls are from Manchester University and are called Deborah and Louise. It turns out that Deborah is in lodgings with a girl called Diane, who is another girl that I was in the same year as, back in Junior school, while Louise performs as a singer in a band that she set up with her boyfriend at Manchester University. Louise is full of fun and a bit cheeky, in a good way, while Deborah is quieter and more studious.

Each day presents new and interesting challenges for the team while the evenings are spent in the bar with my team, watching Andy and Simon trying unsuccessfully to get inside Louise's Knickers. She flirts outrageously and enjoys their attention but has no intention of surrendering herself to their boyish charms.

The course is excellent, and I really enjoy the challenge, but following a week of high intensity work and after- hours socialising, I am ready for a break. I would recommend the course highly and am delighted to have been involved with such a well thought out introduction to a Career for University Graduates. It offered support with Presentation Skills, Decision

Making, Memory Skills, Judgement, Leadership, Communication Skills and how to Work with others, surely most of the attributes that any potential employer will be looking for. The course managed to make working for a living sound like fun and there wasn't an arsehole in sight, so I must be starting to mellow in my maturity.

I have a quiet one on the Friday night and arrange to see all the lads from Leigh on Saturday for our final get together, before Mark, Colin and I return to university, for our third and final year. I check the newspaper and see that Rock Hudson has become the first high profile celebrity to die of AIDs, at the age of 59. He was a prominent male lead in the Golden Age of Hollywood and so it has come as a surprise to many that he was gay. He won an academy award for his role in 'Giant' where he acted alongside Elizabeth Taylor and the late James Dean. Hopefully, more money will now be raised to support AIDs research to find a cure for this terrible disease.

Manchester United fail to win for the first time in the League this season when they draw 1-1 with Luton Town, but they are still playing incredibly well, and the dream is still on.

For our big Saturday night out, we decide to have a change of tempo and visit the Eagle and Hawk pub, which is a little walk from the centre of Leigh, just past the Police Station and before St Joseph's R.C Church. We need a proper catch up after what has been a hectic summer and the Eagle and Hawk will offer us the right ambience to do this.

Tony is single again after splitting up with Susan, who proved that she was a bit of a minx by sleeping with another bloke on holiday. She might have got away with it, if Tony's sister hadn't been on the same holiday, sharing a room, but when you're young, you're daft.

This means that the six of us are all single again, just as we were twelve months ago, when my story began. I think it is fair to say that we are all a little more battle hardened than we were twelve months ago and have all done some growing up. Only Mark seems to be the same bloke as he was twelve months ago, and this somehow feels strangely comforting.

While playing pool in the back room of the pub we talk about girls, sport, politics and music before getting onto the big news story about Rock Hudson dying of AIDs. We probably aren't the go-to guys in Leigh when it comes to the latest trends and fashions, but we do know what is going on in the news and are more aware than most about the increasing rhetoric regarding the threat being posed by AIDs. We talk about the misconceptions on the subject, the stories of how it can be transmitted, and the finger pointing that is taking place, but no-one here is blaming anyone. Well, apart from Tony who blames the 'sad fucker in Africa who shagged a monkey'. We know, as young men, we could be one bad decision away from a potential death sentence and we are all a little wary. Most of us are sensible, but we all like a few pints and I know as well as anyone what situations a person can find themselves in after a heavy night of drinking. The truth is, if you sleep with one person 'unprotected' you are essentially sleeping with every person that they have slept with and then every person that they have slept with etc. Everyone has a story to tell and Chris talks about his worries about the Blood Transfusion he had

3 years ago, as a result of his illness. Only Paul is quiet on the subject and seems to be concentrating on his pool, which probably explains why he keeps winning tonight. He is about to take his shot on the black when he looks up and says to no-one in particular.

"You know I'm gay, right?"

All the lads look at one another and only Tony looks visibly shocked.

"About fucking time", I say, laughing. "I thought you were never going to tell us".

"What gave it away?", says Paul grinning?

"The Eurovision party", says Chris.

"That big hole in your arse" says Colin.

"So, where is Desmond tonight?", says Mark.

"We split up", says Paul miserably, "he was cheating on me with someone from the gym, apparently, it's been going on for months".

"Bummer", says Colin, and everyone laughs.

Mark and I are to return to Salford tomorrow in preparation for our third and final year at university. I have more reason than most to be cheerful, having already completed 5/11ths of my final Degree and another 2/11ths is to be taken up with my dissertation. I do need to start giving my dissertation some serious consideration as it needs to be completed by the end of the Christmas break, but I would sooner be writing about a subject of my choosing rather than taking another couple of exams next summer. I haven't yet decided about the subject of my dissertation, and this will need to be my top priority next week. At least I won't be having any more girlfriend issues this term.

CHAPTER 15.
'IT IS WHAT IT IS'
October 7th – 13th November 1985.

For our 3rd year at university Mark and I are in the same flat at Larch Court with Nick, but Mike has moved on to be with his like -minded, Christian friends. I will miss Mike being at the flat with us, but he has promised to visit us from time to time. This, however, means there will be a fourth, yet unknown person, joining us.

We hear on the news that P.C Keith Blakelock of the London Metropolitan Police force has been fatally stabbed during rioting at Broadwater Farm Housing Estate in Tottenham. The riot started when a black lady named Cynthia Jarrett died of a heart attack while her home was being searched by police. Keith Blakelock was in attendance to protect fire fighters who were themselves under attack. When he stumbled and fell, he was surrounded by a group of about 50 people and received over 40 injuries inflicted by machetes and other weapons. He had a six- inch-long knife in his neck, buried up to the hilt. He was only 40 years old and married with 3 sons. The 3 of us watch the news in disbelief, horrified that this has happened in the U.K. I can understand how some communities can feel victimised by the police and sometimes feel the need to lash out. I realise that prejudices exist in all areas of society, whether it be due to Race, Colour, Religion, Gender, Sexuality or to Class, but this kind of violence solves nothing. This only proves that the perpetrators involved in the murder are dangerous fucking animals, that need to be caged up for the rest of their sad and sorry lives. I go to bed feeling upset and angry and think of the policeman's family getting the awful news of his death, before discovering that his death was far worse than they could ever have imagined. The bastards that did this are 'fucking scum' who place no value on human life and should be treated in the same manner when they are arrested and locked up.

My first week back in Salford requires a decision on the title of my dissertation and I have decided that it will be focused on British history between the 2 World Wars. I have often wondered why Britain hasn't had the same revolutionary tendencies of other European countries, particularly considering the terrible poverty that existed between the 2 World Wars, and so I propose this topic to my tutor, as the subject of my dissertation. I will aim to focus on the Political Parties of the time, including the rise of the Labour Party and Fascism and look at the Poverty and Mass Unemployment that could have potentially resulted in a British Revolution.

During the week, I bump into Karen from the Careers course and arrange to have a meal out with her. There is no romance on the cards with Karen, but she is a nice person, and it will be good to have a bit of female company, without the attraction or the distraction.

On Thursday, two icons of the screen die on the same day. Orson Welles, who is considered one of the greatest and influential filmmakers of all time having co -wrote, produced, directed and starred in 'Citizen Kane' in 1941, died of a heart attack at the age of 70. Yul Brynner who was best known for his portrayal of King Mongkut in 'The King and I' died of lung cancer at the age of 65 after 53 years of heavy smoking. Ricky Wilson of the B52's died 2 days later of AIDs at the age of 32.

Manchester United get back to winning ways with a 2-0 victory over Queens Park Rangers and remain well clear at the top of the First Division table. The Social Sciences play their first game of the season and manage to edge an eleven goal, thriller.

We also find out that our 4th flat mate is a second -year student called Rob who comes from Herefordshire. We have taken him to the pub twice and it is already evident that he is a 'tight arse' and a bit of a 'nob-head'. He is determined to become the first student in the history of students that manages to make a profit from his student grant, but if this makes him happy, then good luck to him.

On Wednesday, England beat Turkey 5-0, with a hat-trick from Gary Lineker and it is encouraging to see a decent striker coming good for the National team and hopefully we can look forward to a reasonable World Cup Finals in Mexico next year.

On Saturday, I decide to cook for Karen rather than going out for a meal and make plans to prepare Nick's famous 'Spaghetti Bolognese' for her taste buds. After a delicious meal served with a bottle of cheap red wine from the Co-op, we attend a student party that John has told me about. I quickly remember why I don't attend student parties and I'm pleased that Karen is of the same opinion. They are boring and pretentious and crammed with students boasting about how 'wasted' they are, and how they have already spent Daddy's grant money. I look over at John, standing with some of his flat mates, and while he will be as bored as me, he manages to hide it better. Karen and I decide to leave, quickly say our goodbyes to a couple of random people who may or may not live in the flat and go to the Church pub for a proper drink. As predicted, there is no sense of attraction from either of us, but the conversation is good, and we have a pleasant evening.

Manchester United manage a 1-1 draw with Liverpool at Anfield, and our unbeaten run continues, against probably our greatest threat for this year's title. Unfortunately, the Social Sciences teams unbeaten run comes to an end, when we field a depleted team against the geography boys. Mark turns out for us at left back and following a couple of hefty tackles it is apparent why he prefers playing rugby. The score ends up 4-2 which isn't a bad result considering.

My studies are going well this term and I am on track with both my essays and my tutorial work. My dissertation is still proving to be something of a headache but with plenty of ideas and no words on paper, I am just waiting for that necessary moment of inspiration.

The following weekend I go back to Leigh to meet up with Tony for a couple of drinks. He's not been well due to a touch of shingles on his face, which can be very sore and painful. Tony's been working at the bank for 2 years now and is a hard worker, so I'm suspecting he is suffering from stress. He is a company man now and gone are the cynical comments about his bosses and the hypocritical ways that the bank treats its loyal customers. He wants to be one of the 'young gun's,' and his mindset has had to change to enable him to do this. I admire him and wish him all the best in his endeavours, as this is the way of the world now and you either comply or be pushed towards the door. Fortunately, his sense of humour hasn't completely deserted him, and he's probably got a few party years left in him before he settles down with a wife and mortgage.

Manchester United beat Chelsea 2-1 at Stamford Bridge and with 12 wins, 2 draws and no defeats, the dream season continues. However, the winter months are ahead of us, and we have a number of small, nippy players who might struggle on the heavier pitches, so Mark and I have gathered- together our chickens, but we aren't counting them yet.

I see Elaine and her friends in the Tropics on Sunday evening, and she confirms the venue for her 21st birthday party, next weekend. We are all invited but Tony has a family do next week and Colin won't be back from university, so it will just be Chris, Mark, Paul and I. Sadly, Chris will be in some need of cheering up because he heard last night that Jules has got engaged to a bloke called Malcolm from Bolton. He is well over her by now, but it must have felt like one final stab to his heart, as Jules moves on with her life, with a fiancé.

A couple of days before the party the two miners who killed the taxi driver have their sentences reduced to 8 years for manslaughter.

As the day of Elaine's 21st birthday party arrives I am in a good frame of mind, and I feel that I am functioning well. Life is back to a steady pace without any major drama and my performance levels at university are high. I am not aware of any issues with my second- year exams, and I can feel proud of this considering the mind-blowing trauma that I was going through at the time. In truth, I am probably fortunate to still be in the game. I haven't heard anything more from Bev and have successfully moved on without further contact, putting the whole experience down as a valuable life lesson.

The four of us meet at the Britannia for a few pints before arranging a taxi to Elaine's party. Mark and I are in a good mood following Manchester United's thirteenth win of the season, a 2-0 victory over Coventry City. Chris heard today that he has been promoted at work and Paul is looking fit and well despite his split with Teabag last month. Paul is dressing much better than he was last year, and the muscles are now bulging out of his tee shirt, so I don't think he will be single for long. The transformation from last year is amazing and since he has come out as gay to his family and friends, he is a far more confident and happy human being. I can't imagine the courage it must have taken to be true to himself, in what is a very tough working- class environment, so I have only the utmost respect for Paul. It seems ludicrous that until 1967 (during our lifetime) it was still a criminal offence in England and Wales for two consenting men to commit homosexual acts in the privacy of their own homes. In fact, Scotland did not follow suit until 1980 and Northern Ireland until 1982. The Sexual Offences Act of 1967 stipulated that private sex acts would no longer be a criminal offence for consenting men over the age of 21 and so Paul in accepting his sexuality at the tender age of 20 has been breaking the current law of the land. Fortunately, we do live in an increasingly more tolerant society considering that 'Buggery' as it was politely known, was still a capital crime until 1861 when its punishment was downgraded to life imprisonment. Happy days!

Back in 1985, everyone seems chilled, and ready for a good night and when Patrick tells us that our taxi has arrived, we down our pints and quickly make our way out of the pub.

We arrive at the venue just after 8 o'clock and the encounter happens almost immediately. As I walk towards the bar the D.J is attempting to kick-start the dancing. He has Elaine and her father, Danny, on the dance floor, and after his signal they are required to separate, and go and pick someone else to dance with. This routine should continue until the dance floor is full. I heard the first signal and turned to see Elaine dragging her brother onto the dance floor while her father walked over to a pretty, young woman, wearing a blue dress. It was Beverley. It hadn't even crossed my mind that she would be at the party, and I watched in complete shock as she danced with Danny. Before I was over the shock of seeing her, the D.J made another signal and Bev walked directly over to me and held out her left arm. I hesitated, but only momentarily, as everyone was still watching who was being chosen for dance duties and I had a responsibility to keep the party going.

"Hello" she said, "How are you?"

I tried to speak, but nothing came out.

"I was really upset when you didn't invite me to your 21st birthday party" she said.

"What are you talking about", I uttered, "We aren't together anymore".

"I know, but I would have come with Eileen, and I did send you a card".

This was typical Bev speak and I was becoming wise to it. I was about to ask her what game she was playing, but the D.J made his signal and we had to part ways. I walked over to the side of the dance floor and picked the first woman I came across to carry on the dancing but sat down as soon as the song finished.

"Was that Bev?", said Mark. "What's she doing here?"

"She must have been invited by Eileen", I say.

"Did you know she was coming?"

"Does it look like, I knew?"

"Shit", he says, "What are you going to do?"

"Get pissed", I say.

"Sounds like a plan", replies Mark, "I'm in".

Paul wanders over and asks the same questions as Mark.

"I'll get another round in", says Paul.

I sit and stare across the dance floor at Bev sitting amongst a group of girls with Eileen by her side. Her dress is more conservative compared with her usual attire, but she still looks amazing.

"You can't go through that crap again", says Mark, gulping his pint.

"I've no intention of having anything more to do with her", I say, unconvincingly.

"I wonder what time the buffet opens", says Mark, "I'm starving".

Elaine comes over to ask me about Bev. "I didn't realise that you two were still in touch".

"We aren't", I say agitated by all the questions.

"Oh, I see", says Elaine, slightly taken aback.

Bev suddenly appeared at our table by Elaine's side.

"Can we talk", she asks.

"I think we'd better", I say in a determined manner.

"Get her told", whispers Mark, as I stand up.

We find a free table and I ask the first question. "What game are you playing, Bev?"

"No game", says Bev, "I just wanted to see you".

"About what", I say, bewildered by her calm manner.

"I felt we left things on a bad note", she says.

"You did the dirty on me and you have another boyfriend".

"I know", she says, "but he's not you".

"Wasn't that the whole point, Bev?" "You preferred him over me".

"I never said that I preferred him, he was just different".

"Bev, we were supposed to be in love, you don't do that to someone you care for".

"I know", she says, "Let me make it up to you".

"How on earth are you going to do that?"

"What are you doing tomorrow,", she says.

"I'm going back to Salford",

"Ok, go back in the morning and I'll come with you".

"Seriously", I say.

"Why not, I'll pack my bags for Liverpool and come with you until Monday, instead".

"You want to stop over in Salford, tomorrow night"?

"Yes, if that's ok with you?"

"What about your boyfriend?"

"He doesn't need to know".

"Fantastic", I say ironically, "Is this how you treat people now?"

"Can I come with you, or not?"

"I'll be at Leigh Bus Station at 10.30, if you want to come, I won't stop you."

I stand up and walk back to the lads table and sit down next to Mark.

"All sorted", says Mark.

"Yes", I say, "she's coming to Salford and stopping over tomorrow night".

"You really told her then" says Mark sarcastically. "This is not going to end well".

I briefly considered whether Bev would show up the following morning, but I knew she would. This was her kind of thing, and she was already waiting when I arrived. I had planned to be cool about what we were doing but did need to ask her about the state of her relationship with Graham.

"Oh, it's ok", she responded nonchalantly, "but we're not sleeping together at the moment".

"So, you've fallen out then?"

"No, I don't think he's that bothered about sex".

"What am I then, your stud?"

"If you want it, the jobs yours", she says grinning.

"Just two friends hooking up for sex", I say, feeling exasperated by the whole conversation.

"That's right", she replies, satisfied.

By the time that we arrive at the flat in Salford, we don't even stop for a drink. Rob is sitting in the kitchen with a friend, eating a jam butty.

"Hi", I say, while passing the kitchen door and running up the stairs with Bev. She takes off her top and starts to unzip her jeans, while I do the same. There are no tender touches, no preamble, no whispers of ever- lasting love, just pure unadulterated lust for one another. She is already wet, and I am deep inside her in a moment. She moans loudly, closing her eyes and biting her lip.

"Fuck, yes", she utters, as I go at it like a Tommy gun in a gangster movie. There are no pleasantries spoken, just moans, sighs and curses, and then we make like two 100 metre sprinters, pressing hard to be first past the line, but ending with a photograph finish.

"Shit, I've missed that", says Bev.

"Great, you can go home now", I say.

"Don't be nasty", that's horrible, she says.

"Sorry", I say, "but I still have a few issues getting my head around this".

"It is, what it is", says Bev.

"Ok", I say, "but at some point, you're going to need to clarify."

I go downstairs briefly to make us a drink and something to eat but we stay in bed for the rest of the night. Bev is up early the following morning to catch the bus through to Liverpool.

"I can be back with you at about 6 o'clock, next Friday", says Bev, walking towards the front door.

"Oh, so we're doing this again", I say.

"What's a girl to do", comes her reply, "I just can't keep my hands off you".

"Will your boyfriend have anything to say on the matter?"

"He's away with the T.A next weekend", she says. "He's on manoeuvres or something in Scotland. I'll probably stay over until Tuesday or Wednesday; if that's ok?"

"I do have a few things on next weekend", I say, knowing this will make no difference to Bev, "but I suppose we can work around that".

"Great", she says, "that's a date". And she is gone.

Alain Prost wins the World Drivers' Championship with Ayrton Senna finishing 4th and Nigel Mansell 6th and I start to read Madame Bovary by Victor Hugo.

I wander down to Castle Irwell on the Wednesday to watch an organised Bonfire and have a catch up with Karen. I tell her that Bev is coming over for the weekend just in case she sees us together. Karen knows all about Bev and doesn't seem heartbroken.

Bev arrives on Friday as planned and I have arranged to take some local kids ice skating with John on Saturday morning. I have never tried ice skating before, but I've done roller skating with Chris at the Bolton indoor rink on Sunday nights, when I was 16 and while my skill is limited, my balance is good. Unfortunately, John lacks both skill and balance and spends most of the time on his arse. The kids take to the skating very well and appreciate their time on the rink.

While I am away from the flat Bev gets on with some work and chats to Rob, who never seems to go out.

On the way home I pick up a couple of tickets for a band that is playing at the University tonight. There are rumours that it is the band 'Mud' who were big in the early 70's and it will be a blast from the past for me. I used to like the Glam Rock era when I was a kid with T. Rex and Sweet being my favourite bands. Gary Glitter has already performed at the University, but for some reason, he had to keep sitting down during his set. I see a copy of Lolita at the University bookshop, but I don't buy it. Manchester United lose their first game of the season against Sheffield Wednesday and I am convinced that Bev is a bad omen.

Bev and I go to the Saturday night gig to find out that it isn't Mud playing tonight, but they are due at the University soon. It is a little disappointing because I have been practising my 'Tiger Feet' dance since I got back to the flat. I offer to do the dance for Bev, but she doesn't seem interested in my feet. We talk to John for a while and bump into Karen, but we largely stay on our own throughout the evening. I try to broach what will happen after Bev goes back to Liverpool on Wednesday, but she isn't ready to talk about that yet.

There is no football game on Sunday, so Bev and I have a lie in and then set off for a walk around the University grounds. We stop off for a drink at Castle Irwell, but it is eerily quiet, and I don't see anyone I know. There is plenty of sex over the next few days but it's clear that there is something missing from our relationship, and I think they call it love.

It is Tuesday night when I again bring up the subject of where we are going with whatever 'this' is, and Bev realises that we cannot avoid the subject any longer.

"I think I need to have a talk with Graham", she says, miserably.

"Ok", I say, "and what will you talk about?"

"I'll tell him where I've been this weekend and he will probably finish with me".

"And that's your plan", I say, feeling the anger build inside me. "You're actually going to let him make the decision for you?"

"Well, what else can I do?"

"I think you need to stop acting like a petulant child and make your own mind up". "You have a decision to make now, and If you don't, I will make it for you".

Bev starts to become upset, but I cannot make this easy for her.

"Do you want us to get back together?", she says.

"I'll be honest with you, Bev, I still fancy you like crazy, but I no longer love you. You've hardened me up, and I don't think I can ever trust you again. In fact, I'm not sure I will trust anyone again after what you have put me through. I feel like I'm a different person, since meeting you. What we are doing now, is plain wrong".

"Ok", she says, "I will speak with Graham tomorrow night and tell him it's over".

"How will I know how you've got on? Do you want me to come with you?"

"No, you will only scare him, he's smaller than you. I will write to you afterwards and let you know how it went. He won't harm me, so don't worry."

I walk to the bus stop with Bev on Wednesday morning to see her off to Liverpool. She looks sad at the prospect of having to give up one of her men.

If she puts a letter in Thursday's post, I should know how things have gone by Saturday morning. I really don't think I will be too disappointed if she decides to stay with Graham again, and I'm prepared for that to happen. I am, however, worried about how he might react when he finds out where she has been over the past week. You can only push a person so far before they crack, and I wonder if Bev is about to see another side of Graham.

That night, Mark and I watch England and Northern Ireland play out a drab 0-0 draw in a World Cup Qualifier where both teams have already qualified for next year's tournament. Mark seems pleased that Bev has left the flat and while he has been perfectly civil to her while she has been here, he thinks she is trouble and wants her out of my life forever. As a good friend, he is undoubtedly worried for me, but I assure him that I am fine and will be ok this time, whatever happens next. He seems dubious over my assurances, but I know he will support me whatever I decide to do. After the game ends Mark puts on 'Something better change' by the Stranglers and turn up the volume to the 'too loud' button. We try to do some head banging, but it just gives us neck ache.

CHAPTER 16
NO SLEEP IN DUBLIN.
November 16th – December 12th, 1985.

On Saturday, Manchester United draw 0-0 with Spurs and unsurprisingly there is no letter in the post from Bev. I am unconcerned at this point and just get on with life. The term is still going well from an academic point of view and my only minor concern continues to be my dissertation. I have managed to secure a selection of useful books from the library and have begun to form an idea in my mind as to how the chapters might flow but Mark is now of the opinion that I am destined never to commit my masterpiece to paper.

On Monday, Nick tells Mark and I about a trip he has booked for the weekend with Ian and Richard and wants to know if we want to join them. They have arranged to go on the overnight ferry to Dublin on Friday night, spending the day in Dublin and then returning on the Saturday night ferry, thus avoiding any accommodation costs. Mark has a couple of concerts to attend in Manchester on the run up to Christmas and is saving his money for those. However, I have a word with John, and he is keen to join us on the trip. John now has a new girlfriend who 'picked him up' in the library. She is beautiful and a massive upgrade on his last girlfriend, if only because she is a much nicer human being. I make sure that he is comfortable in leaving her for the weekend and we go and book our tickets for the ferry. The only concern we have with the trip is the football match we have arranged for Sunday morning, by which time we will not have slept for 2 days. It is said that sleeping is for wimps, but we decide to go on the trip anyway.

Still no letter has arrived from Bev, so I am starting to wonder whether she is ok after her discussion with Graham. Of course, it is more than possible that she hasn't even spoken to Graham about our weekends together, so I refuse to get myself worked up over the situation.

We catch the coach to Liverpool on Friday night and take the crossing over to Dublin. There are no cabins available for us to sleep in as part of the cost, so we have a few beers and crash out on the floor. In March of this year the first major international conference was held in Villach, Austria, to discuss the 'greenhouse effect' which has led many scientists to believe that temperatures on earth are steadily rising as a direct result of man's lack of respect for our planet. It is predicted that during the first half of the next century, greenhouse gases will cause a rise in global temperatures greater than any in man's history. Gases such as CO_2, methane, ozone, CFC's and nitrous oxide will all contribute to this global warming. While this is obviously a concern for the future of our planet, I can't help wishing it would get a move on, because its fucking freezing tonight.

On the trip over to Dublin we discuss Mark's get rich idea that he shared with Nick and I this week. It sounds like a good plan, but we need some money behind us to make it successful. On Wednesday, the Windows 1.0 operating system was released by a company called Microsoft which was co- founded by entrepreneurs Bill Gates and Paul Allen in 1976. Mark has been following developments in the world of computing for many years and thinks that we all need to buy shares when the company goes public next year. Apparently, Windows 1.0 provides its users with the ability to work on several programs at the same time while being able to switch easily between them. I have absolutely no idea what he is talking about, but Mark assures us that the technology is amazing, and that buying enough shares will make us into millionaires by the time we are 30. To showcase their operating system, Microsoft have teamed up with IBM who are currently the world's leading supplier of computer equipment to commercial enterprises. This will help to raise their prestige and transform Microsoft into one of the leading software producers in the world. I am more tempted by Mark's get rich proposition than Nick, but I have known Mark for longer and if he says I'm going to be a millionaire, I trust him, because Mark knows what he is talking about.

Another company Mark is always talking about is 'Apple' co-founded by Steven Jobs and Steve Wozniak in 1976. They released the Apple Macintosh in January last year with an outstanding television advertisement alluding to George Orwell's 1984. The advertisement was directed by Ridley Scott and starred athlete Anja

Major as the unnamed heroine and David Graham as Big Brother. For trivia buffs Anja Major also played 'Nikita' in Elton John's video for his East German love song, released in September. The Apple Macintosh became the first mass produced computer with a Graphical user interface (GUI) and it has already played a pivotal role in establishing desktop publishing as a general office function. The heart of the computer is a Motorola 68000 microprocessor connected to 128kb Ram, while its beige case consists of a 9- inch monitor with keyboard and mouse. However, Mark is less convinced about the future of 'Apple' because Jobs and Wozniak have both left the company this year, and it is apparent that IBM are way ahead of all their rivals.

I would like to tell you that we spent our time in Dublin exploring Samuel Beckett Bridge, Trinity College, Dublin Castle and O'Connell Bridge, but I would be lying. We did walk by the banks of the river Liffey, but only because we were searching for the next bar to go in.

Dublin has a significant literary history, and I purchased a copy of 'Dubliners' by James Joyce, which is a selection of short stories about certain incidents and characters from the early 20th century. I briefly considered buying Ulysees, instead, but decided that was a far too complicated read for a boys' weekend in Dublin; and was more expensive. Other literary figures from Dublin include Nobel Prize winners William Butler Yeats, George Bernard Shaw and Samuel Beckett. I have already read work by Oscar Wilde, Jonathan Swift and Bram Stoker, so I can at least pretend that I experienced some culture while I was in this marvellous city. I much preferred the wit of Wilde to the heavy going Swift and wasn't really a fan of Bram Stokers Vampire creation. I did, however, enjoy Mary Shelley's Frankenstein, which wonderfully aroused my imagination. As a young boy, I used to watch the Horror Double Bill on BBC2 Saturday night television, while my parents were out at the pub. Again, it was Frankenstein that grabbed my attention, although I did have a weakness for the Werewolf stories. I think I only bothered watching the Vampire stories because they were always biting the necks of virgins and I was curious to see what one looked like.

By mid- afternoon, some of the lads are starting to tire due to too much booze and too little sleep, so we decide to go into the cinema where they are showing an Eddie Murphy Double Bill of 48 hours and Beverley Hills Cop. Ian and Nick use the opportunity to catch up on a bit of shut eye while the rest of us attempt to stay focused on the films. I start to nod off during Beverley Hills Cop, which I have already seen with Bev, and this starts me wondering again about what might have happened since her return to Liverpool, and why she hasn't been in touch. If she has decided to avoid confrontation, the most cowardly solution would be to remain with Graham, and I am well- aware that this is Bev's most likely 'go to option'. However, I cannot rule out that something bad has happened because it is unlikely that the news would filter back to me, when no-one in Leigh knows that we have been seeing each other again.

We leave the cinema before the end of the second film because Ian wants to see the final scores coming in at the pub. Unfortunately, it is bad news for Manchester United as they have lost 3-0 to Leicester

City with 2 goals coming from Alan Smith and one from Gary McAllister. With Gary Lineker having departed for Everton this season, I had suspected that Leicester City would struggle, but it looks as though the talent is still coming through. I quite like Leicester City as a football club, so I'm not devastated by the result, but it does look as though Manchester United's bubble has been well and truly pricked. It is becoming increasingly unlikely that they will be parading the First Division title around Old Trafford next May and so we can only hope for another F.A. Cup success to save our season.

A few pints later and a McDonalds and we are ready to reboard the ferry back to Liverpool. Once reacquainted with the layout of the ship, I find a comfortable chair, open my new book and wait patiently for it to send me to sleep. Richard sits next to me and loads Billy Joel's Greatest hits into his Walkman, puts his ear plugs in and closes his eyes. As it happens, sleep proves impossible for me, and I've read more than half of the book by the time we arrive back in Liverpool. Richard is fast asleep, and I can hear 'Piano Man' softly exuding from his left ear. I gently wake him, and we board the coach back to Salford by which time all five of us are dead on our feet. However, there is a football match to play and so I struggle to get my football kit on and walk slowly down to the ground. I look across at John as the whistle triggers the beginning of the match and he looks how I feel, but he gives me a nod and we go into battle. Somehow, the lads are inspired, and we produce our best performance of the year with a 7-1 victory over the Scientists. John and I are both on the score sheet, but it is Richard that receives the biggest applause of the match with a 30 -yard pile-driver that cannons down off the cross bar and into the back of the net, for his first University goal. We leave the pitch delighted with our efforts, and despite a very brief consideration of going to the pub to celebrate, the 5 happy Dubliners go straight to bed.

By the following weekend there is still no letter from Bev and despite my better efforts I have started to feel a little stressed out. Mark manages to calm me down, but I decide if I haven't heard anything by Thursday, I am going to set off for Liverpool. I have no idea how big Liverpool University is or where Bev is living this year, but I am determined to find her. However, by Thursday, I feel so ill that I abandon all thoughts of looking for Bev in Liverpool and decide to resolve matters when I go home for Christmas.

On the Wednesday Neil Kinnock strangely suspends the Liverpool District Labour Party amid Trotskyist militant group allegations, which I would have thought was a good thing.

On Friday, Gerard Hoare, ex Seychelles leader is assassinated in London, but I can't help wondering what the weather is like in the Seychelles at this time of the year.

Manchester United draw 1-1 at home to Watford on Saturday to continue their run of poor results, but they are still top of the League due to their fantastic start to the season. I manage to get my head down and continue the good work I have undertaken during the term so far, and I now have a structure in place for my Dissertation, which I will probably end up writing during my 4 weeks Christmas Break. Feeling satisfied with our present workloads and a plan in place for the remainder of the term Nick and I decide to accompany

Ian back to Liverpool this weekend. It is good to get away again and I assure Mark that I have no intention of going anywhere near Liverpool University. Instead, we go to watch Liverpool beat Q.P.R 3-0 with goals from Malby, Walsh and Johnson. On leaving Anfield we hear that Manchester United have secured a narrow 1-0 victory over Ipswich Town, but based on the way that Liverpool played today, the signs are ominous as regards them winning the First Division title this season. On Saturday evening the three of us and Jan go into Liverpool and have a fantastic time in a fantastic city. The locals are friendly and extremely entertaining with their quick wit and sarcastic comments. Ian makes me nervous when he tells them who I support, but despite a bit of banter and piss taking over Man United's recent results the atmosphere is good natured without any hint of malice. I notice that 'Letter to Brezhnev' starring Margi Clarke and Alexandra Pigg is showing at the cinema in Liverpool. I hope that whoever wrote the letter isn't expecting a reply because he died 3 years ago. Gorbachev, however, might respond, because he seems like a very nice man.

We return to Salford on Sunday on what is the 5th anniversary of John Lennon's senseless murder at the age of only 40. We can only 'Imagine' what fantastic music he would have created after 1980, having just kick started his career again after spending the previous 5 years bringing up his son Sean.

As the Christmas Break draws closer' I feel relaxed and in control of my life. There has been no blood in my pee for over a month now so I'm hoping that whatever was wrong has now resolved itself, but I'm no medical expert. I keep hearing the Wham song, 'Last Christmas' haunting me, wherever I go, despite it being a year ago since it was in the charts. It was kept off the number one slot by Band Aid and remained stuck at number 2 for 5 weeks. I have a horrible feeling that it is going to be one of those songs played at Christmas for the next 50 years like Slade's 'Merry Christmas Everybody' and Wizzard's 'I wish it could be Christmas Everyday'. In all honesty, I slightly preferred Wizzard's song and was surprised to discover that it only reached number 4 in the charts, when it was released in 1973. It is good to see in 1985 that Roy Wood hasn't aged one bit and he still looks 90. When I get back to Leigh, I think I will dig out my copy of 'See my Baby Jive' which was released by Wizard in May 1973 and did get to Number 1. What I feel we need this Christmas is a Punk Christmas song to reach the Number 1 slot. However, as long as it's not Cliff Richard or that annoying pipsqueak, Aled Jones, with his version of 'Walking in the Air', I don't mind. I just hope his voice breaks soon.

CHAPTER 17
NEW BEGINNINGS
December 13th – December 25th, 1985.

The term ends on Friday 13th December, which might sound a little ominous to most people, but I'm not superstitious, so I crossed myself twice like a good Christian and headed back to Leigh. I had arranged to meet Mark in the Britannia for a couple of pre -Christmas drinks and I took the opportunity to pick his brains on how best to approach the matter of contacting Beverley tomorrow. I hadn't heard anything from her since she left Larch Court to go back to Liverpool in October, but on a positive note, I had become increasingly confident that she wasn't dead. Mark was also sure that Bev was fine but was as clueless as me as how to approach the situation. To be honest, I think Mark thought I should get on with my life and not bother contacting her at all. He was sick and tired of the sound of her name and wanted to enjoy his pint. When Colin and Paul turned up at the pub, the conversation changed to Teabag. Colin wanted to know how Teabag had got his nickname and what it meant. Paul started to laugh and told us that an ex- boyfriend from the States had given him the name about 5 years ago.

"And", said Colin, "what does it mean?"

"I can show you a photo if you like?", said Paul.

"Ok", said Colin, suddenly sounding dubious.

Paul took the photo out of his wallet and handed it over to me to share with Colin and Mark. I looked at the photo and wasn't sure what it was that I was looking at.

"Oh, you dirty fucking pervert", said Colin, suddenly realising what we were all staring at.

"You are one sad fuck; I can't believe you carry a photo of that around with you". Colin snatched the photo out of my hand and threw it back to Paul, who was bent over in hysterics. "I'm going to the bar", said Colin, disgusted by what he had seen.

Paul, still trying not to laugh, carefully described to me and Mark what the term 'teabag' meant, explaining that he had only taken the photo as a joke.

"I can't believe that Boots printed it", said Mark, and we all laughed.

I only had a couple more drinks before heading home early. I wanted to have a clear head in the morning.

On Saturday, I called Bev's home at about 10.30, hoping that she would answer, but it was her mother who picked up the phone. She sounded a little frosty when she realised that it was me but disappeared to go and get Bev. I waited for what seemed like an age until Bev answered sounding tired and weary. She didn't want to talk and didn't want to meet me for a conversation. I remained calm and told her that I wasn't angry and was just relieved that she was ok, but still, she said nothing. I continued to talk calmly to Bev, explaining that I had been expecting a letter from her and deserved to know what had happened following her return to Liverpool from Salford. I had accepted that our relationship was over and told her that I was no longer in love with her, but felt that I needed an explanation, if only to draw a line under the whole matter. Again, she didn't respond, so I went on the attack. I told her that I was happy to come round to the house to see what her mother made of the situation. It wasn't a nice tactic to use, but it worked, and Bev agreed that we should go out for a walk. I picked her up from outside her house in my dad's car, drove around the corner out of sight, and parked up.

Bev did not look well, wore no make- up, and was dressed in an old black track suit. She was already starting to cry and looked as though she would prefer to be anywhere else in the world at this precise moment. I re-iterated that I wasn't angry and just wanted to hear her story. She told me that Graham was furious when she returned to Liverpool and had already worked out where she had been. He hadn't hit her, but he had been angrier than she had ever seen him. Eventually, he had broken down in tears and told her how much he loved her and how he couldn't imagine life without her. I'm sure that emotional blackmail played some part, but I did feel for him, knowing how unintentionally cruel Bev could be. Bev craved excitement and enjoyed falling in love and was always going to be looking for her next fix. She also liked to be the one in control and liked to be in her own comfort zone. I had realised that she was too immature to work on developing love and preferred the thrill of the initial romance to the boring bits that followed. In hindsight, I had been the grown up one all along and the self confidence that she oozed on our first meetings had been the actions of an intelligent articulate girl, rather than a mature young woman. I could now see Bev for what she was and the charming girl that I had put on a pedestal was crumbling before my eyes. She went on to say that it was easier to stay with Graham because he loved her, while I no longer did, and while this sounded a bit simplistic, it was probably true. She said that she had started to write me a letter on numerous occasions but didn't know what to say, in view of her ever-changing mindset. It was the same selfish reasoning of the damaged girl that had slowly started to emerge following the initial euphoria of our relationship, and I knew now that I was better out of it. It would have been easy for Bev to do the right thing by writing to me as promised, but she had chosen not to because it had been difficult for her. At last, I felt relief that the truth was out, and I urged her to try and treat people more thoughtfully, in the future.

"If you have decided that Graham is the man for you, start by showing him some respect and prove that you love him and are committed to the relationship", I say, preparing to drive her home.

"Ok", she says miserably, "but there's something else".

"That's ok", I say, "what is it?".

"I think I'm pregnant", she says.

By this point, I believed that Bev could no longer shock me, but the words hit me like a hammer blow to the head.

"And?", I ask anxiously.

"It's yours!", she says, almost defiantly.

"You said, you thought you were pregnant", I say, trying to remain calm.

"Yes, I need to get confirmation from the doctors, next week, but I'm pretty sure".

"So, why are you assuming that it's mine?" I ask suspiciously.

"Because, I wasn't sleeping with Graham, at the time."

"Does he know you're pregnant?".

"Yes", she says, her eyes starting to fill up with tears again.

"I'm assuming your mum and dad don't know?".

"Are you joking, they'd kill me".

"Ok, calm down", I say, "when are you going to the doctors?"

"I will call on Monday, but I don't know when I will get the results", she replies.

"Do you want me to go to the doctors with you?", I ask sympathetically.

"No, but thanks, I promise to call and let you know the result".

"Ok, try not to worry in the meantime, when will you call me?"

"I will leave it until Friday, is 6 o'clock ok?".

"That's fine, I will make sure that I answer".

With a plan agreed, I turn on the car engine, take Bev back to her parents house, and go home.

During the week, I am calmer than expected, probably because I know that I may need to be the strong one and step up if required. If she is pregnant and I am the father, I don't want to be leaving things for Bev and Graham to sort out, especially if there is a decision to make.

During the week, I read 'Crime and Punishment' by Fydor Dostoevsky, and I am dragged into the existentialist world of Rodion Raskolnikov as he desperately searches to find some meaning to his troubled existence in St Petersburgh. Raskolnikov is cruelly confined by his mind and over analyses every situation, mistrusting the motives of others and feeling alone and isolated. As he considers murdering a pawnbroker that he owes money to, he attempts to justify his actions to himself by thinking of the resulting benefits to others.

It is Soren Kierkegaard that is generally considered to be the first philosopher to propose that the individual 'rather than society or religion' is responsible for giving meaning to life and living it authentically, and while I do agree with him, it's bloody hard work.

I take some time to consider the impact a baby will have on our lives, and it is a scary prospect. I am in little doubt that Bev will decide to terminate the pregnancy, but I need to put all options on the table and give them equal consideration. Bringing a child into the world should not mean that our lives are ruined, just because we are young and still at university. Other, less fortunate people have managed to cope with having a child at a young age and we would have plenty of family support to assist us. There is of course, 'the elephant in the room'.

Bev is currently dating another man who 'allegedly' is not the father of the baby.

It is sad and unfortunate that I can't be completely certain that Bev isn't lying. However, I cannot imagine what her reasons would be for lying.

I update Mark on my current predicament and tell Chris when he phones up regarding a night out on Friday. While Mark is predictably shocked, Chris remains calm, and says it is best not to worry about it until after the phone call. He also offers his ear if I need someone to talk to after the phone call on Friday. I thank Chris for his kind offer and promise that I will ring him when everything becomes clear.

Friday, at 6 o'clock arrives and the telephone rings immediately. The doctor has confirmed that Beverley is not pregnant. The relief in Bev's voice is evident and she sounds much calmer than when I last spoke to her. Bev agrees to meet up in Leigh tomorrow afternoon so that she can give me the full story, rather than whispering it over the phone. I call Chris to tell him the good news and arrange to meet him at the Britannia at 8 o'clock.

It is a reduced turn out tonight with Tony poorly again and Colin on a date with a young lady. The weather is awful, so we decide to remain in the Britannia for the evening. It is Christmas next week, so we take it easy and have a catch up. Paul isn't his usual cheerful self and goes home early with the promise that he will be in a better frame of mind for the Christmas Eve Party at the Boars Head. While Mark is doing his best to chat up Charlie, Chris asks how I am feeling now that I have received Bev's news. I tell him that I am pleased that the relationship is over, but I still feel a sense of loss, from what was my first Love.

"I can understand that", says Chris, "It will probably hurt for a while, but it's called 'first love' for a reason".

"Why's that", I say, wondering where Chris is going with this.

"Because there is a better, 'true love' to follow", he says. "You might decide you want to take a bit of a break from dating like I did, or you could meet your true love tomorrow, only time will tell".

"Jules really hurt you, didn't she mate?"

"She did Adam, and I wasn't sure that I was going to get over it, but I have, and I'm stronger for it. I'm enjoying life again and I'm well settled in Leigh, but I'm not sure its where your destiny lies".

"You don't think I'll stay in Leigh?", I ask, surprised.

"I don't think you've found your chosen path in life, yet", says Chris. "You may find your calling lies elsewhere next summer, because I think you've outgrown Leigh, much the same as you've outgrown Bev. You're a clever bloke, Adam, with a good grasp on how the world works, and I think your future can be as remarkable as you want it to be".

I get home feeling reasonably sober, with the words of Chris still ringing in my ears. I think about what it must have been like for Chris during his illness and I am pleased that he has emerged from his nightmare as a stronger and better man.

The following afternoon, Bev acts as though the weight of the world has been taken off her shoulders, but she still looks poorly and a little too thin. Graham wants to stand by Bev despite her recent transgressions and she has agreed to be a better girlfriend. I have my doubts, but I am not going to tell her that and it is none of my business anymore. We talk about our plans for Christmas Eve and for the Christmas period and do a little shopping, exchanging small gifts as a parting gesture. I receive a sparkling new 1986 diary to record all the years events, in what will hopefully be a less traumatic twelve months. Despite the pain caused over the second half of our relationship, I will forever remember that wonderful Sunday night in September 1984 when I first met Bev and my world changed forever. I know that I have matured and grown as a person as a result of our meeting, and while I still see the world as a hostile place, I think I am now better equipped to deal with it.

Two days later it is Christmas Eve and tonight I am wearing my blue jeans with a white open necked shirt and a navy- blue cotton jacket. I pop into see my mum before departing and she is sitting on the edge of the bed with her head down. She looks up as I approach, and I can see that she has been crying. She tells me that she is fine, and I have not to worry because she is just being silly. I sit with her for a while and hold her hands which are clasped tight like two little balls, and I can almost feel her pain. She finally tells me that she has packed a bag in case she needs to go to hospital, but she isn't ill and will snap out of it tomorrow. I can feel from her hands that she is anxious, and I manage to open them out and massage them gently until she starts to relax. She lets out a huge sigh and manages to laugh and cry at the same time, before thanking me and telling me not to say anything to my dad. I tell her that I am happy to stay home tonight and watch some television with her, but she won't have it and stands up and walks with me to the bedroom door. I give her a big cuddle and tell her that I love her and that we can talk again tomorrow. My mum thanks me and goes into the bathroom to wash her face before going downstairs with me and waving me off.

Tonight, all the lads are out to celebrate Christmas Eve in style. We have tickets for a party night at the new Boars Head pub extension called Shergars, and

Colin is the first to arrive at the venue, shortly followed by me. He tells me all the details of his date last week. Her name is Theresa, and he has arranged to meet her again on Boxing Day. Apparently, she is the fiancé of a rugby mate of his, so I can't see that ending well. Paul arrives next and tells us that he has heard from a friend at the gym that Teabag hasn't been well and has been absent from work for the past 3 weeks. I just hope that its nothing too serious. Mark and Chris arrive together and while Mark sits down next to Colin, Chris is already talking to a girl at the bar. Her name is Sam, and she is a good- looking girl. Sam has shiny auburn hair that she is wearing up, a nice toothy smile and is impeccably dressed in a figure hugging black and white dress. She is already staring at Chris with that wide eyed look that Bev used to give me, while he is more animated than I have seen him for a long time. Maybe, after our chat last Friday, he has decided that it is time to move on with his love life.

I am wondering where Tony is when he turns up with something of a surprise for me. He has come along with a date called Sandie and she has brought along her best friend, Maria. It is the same Maria that I have met on two previous occasions and once more she looks incredible and walks towards me with a wide smile that shows off her perfect white teeth.

"Hello Adam", she says, "Remember me?"

"I do, what are you doing here?"

"I've come to see you", she replies, with a giggle.

The 4 of us take a table together and Tony does the introductions. Sandie works with Tony and Maria at the bank and is a single mother like Maria, with a two-year-old girl called Natalie. Tony is sporting his new spectacles and has some good news to share. He has passed his Banking Qualifications and is to begin the New year as a qualified Financial Adviser for the Bank.

"Onwards and upwards", he says proudly.

"What's with the glasses", I say.

"Too much reading", says Tony, "It will be you needing them next".

"Nah, perfect vision, me", I say.

"I think you'd suit glasses Adam", says Maria, studying my face.

"Really?", I say, surprised.

"Yes, not sure about the tash though", she says, laughing.

"Is that a subtle way of saying 'get rid'?"

"I might have to make it one of my New Year's Resolutions".

"She doesn't do subtle", says Sandie, "always direct and to the point, our Maria".

"You make me sound awful, it was only a suggestion", says Maria.

"How's Jenny", I say, changing the subject.

"She's doing really well, thanks for asking, she's a little angel".

"And the new home, are you settled in now?"

"It's more of a gradual evolution, we are always so busy".

"And she's started her Banking qualifications as well", says Tony.

"Wow", I say, "how do you find the time?"

"Every second counts", says Maria, laughing. "It's like a military operation getting everything planned out. I can't remember the last time I sat down to watch the television".

"Sandie's the same", said Tony, "she never stops".

"What are you going to do when you finish University, Adam?", asks Sandie.

"I'll probably join you guys at the bank", I say with a wry smile.

"You do realise that you'll have to work and take exams at the same time", Tony says sarcastically.

"Leave him alone", says Maria, defending my honour.

"You started it with the 'tash' comment", says Tony laughing.

And the banter continues, until Tony is talking mainly to Sandie, and I am talking to Maria. She is more serious than Bev and more varied in her topics of conversation. She went to visit Auschwitz in October and is planning on seeing Budapest in the Spring. Maria likes to get out and about when she is able; but doesn't like to take advantage of her Mum and Dad. She loves Motown music and hates Punk, but she does like the Smiths. She is aware that I read a lot and asks me about the authors I have read. She read Pride and Prejudice at school and very much admires the writing of Jane Austen. Maria seems to have a genuine interest in history and enjoys films based on true stories. She supports Manchester United but doesn't know much about football and she thinks that I am very mature for my age. Maria admires Margaret Thatcher and thinks she is doing a good job under the circumstances and while she does feel sorry for the miners, thinks that it is important that the country gets back on its feet. She doesn't have any time for religion. Her daughter, Jenny is her most important priority, but she would like to find love again. I am blown away by her candour and think we have already discussed a greater variety of subjects than during the whole of my relationship with Bev. She isn't trying to be intelligent, she isn't trying to impress, she isn't trying to be sexy, but she is managing all these things, by being herself. There are no mind games being played and no childish antics, but she is sharp, and she is funny. This is a woman who is already living her best life and she seems to like me.

A Diana Ross song is played, and she insists that I dance with her. She kisses me for the first time during 'I'm your man' by Wham and wishes me a Merry Christmas. She thinks that I dress nicely and compliments me on the way I am dressed tonight. I tell her that I thought she was out of my league when we first met; and find it hard to believe that we are now dancing together. Maria tells me that she liked me immediately and that it isn't all about looks. I am not sure whether to be flattered or insulted. I look across at Chris who is dancing with Samantha, and he gives me a wink. Tony is also up dancing with Sandie, and he is whispering something in her ear. Paul is talking to a good- looking guy at the bar while Mark and Colin appear to be deep in conversation. Maria tells me that she is going to be busy with her family over the next few days, but I am welcome to go over to her house on New Year's Eve, after Jenny has gone to bed. We have been drinking wine throughout the evening, and I realise that I'm far from drunk, despite being intoxicated by Maria. She has also been sensible, with Christmas Day now less than an hour away. It's clear that Maria knows what she wants from life, and I get the feeling that she is looking for someone with the same values and a similar outlook on life. Tonight, is my opportunity to make an impression.

At the end of a perfectly civilised night, the girls need to get home to relieve their babysitters and Maria and I exchange numbers. I thank her for a lovely evening and would like to take up her offer of spending New Year's Eve with her. I say that I will call her on Boxing Day to see how Christmas has gone and maybe arrange to go for a walk. I feel as though I have transformed from young man to adult during the evening and realise that if I am going to be Maria's boyfriend, then I need to start behaving more responsibly.

Maria and I kiss goodnight, and she steps into her taxi with Sandie, leaving Tony and I standing by the side of the road.

"Good night?", asks Tony, smiling.

"Amazing", I say, "Am I dreaming?"

"No, for some reason, she really likes you. So don't fuck it up", says Tony.

"I'll try my best", I say, and bid Tony goodnight.

I walk towards Pennington Park and see Chris walking on the other side of the road with Samantha. They are laughing and look great together and it could be the start of a beautiful new relationship. Chris is a good man and deserves someone special in his life.

I take a moment to think about my own blossoming relationship with Maria, still shell shocked that someone so beautiful would want to spend time with me. I am excited at what the future has in store for us but realise that there is still a part of me that needs to lie with the phoenix, if I am to resurrect myself from the ashes, and become the man that I am supposed to be. I now feel ready to make that final transition and move forward with my life. Today, I will spend time with my family, and tomorrow I will get cracking on my dissertation, with a view to having it finished by New Year's Eve. Then I can focus on what I want to achieve in 1986. In just 9 months' time I could be graduated and ready to start work for a FTSE Top 10 company, living a life full of endless possibilities.

I am disturbed from my thoughts by the sound of running coming from behind me and I turn to see if it is someone I know. It is a small skinny bloke with black hair and a moustache. At first it looks as though he is going to run by me, but in an instance, he veers quickly towards me and pokes me in the stomach.

"That's for knocking up me bird", he says in a thick Liverpudlian twang.

I continue to watch him running up the road towards Pennington Park and try to process his words.

Did he say, "knocking up his bird?"

My stomach is starting to throb, and I look down to see that my white shirt is covered in blood. I start to feel a little faint and drop down to my knees, becoming mesmerised by the blood pouring out from beneath my shirt and between my fingers. I begin to feel cold and tired with a desperate urge to lie down and go to sleep. I hear voices and look up to see Mark who is pressing his hands over mine. He is shouting at me, telling me to stay with him, but I just want to close my eyes. The last thing I hear are sirens and then nothing.

THE END.